Gulf

Books by Robert Westall

ROBERT WESTALL

Gulf

EGMONT

For my friend Norma Pitfield,
who hates all war.

First published in Great Britain 1992
by Methuen Children's Books Ltd
Reissued 2002
by Egmont Books Ltd
239 Kensington High Street, London W8 6SA

ISBN 1 4052 0090 1

10 9 8 7 6 5 4 3 2 1

A CIP catalogue record for this title is available from the
British Library

Typeset by Avon DataSet Ltd, Bidford on Avon, Warwickshire
Printed and bound in Great Britain by Cox & Wyman

Contents

One

Birth

I loved my brother. Right from the start. But did I love him enough? I *used* him. You shouldn't *use* people you love. Maybe what happened to him was all my fault . . .

It certainly wasn't my parents' fault. They were smashing parents, and still are, though they don't laugh now like they used to. In the beginning, they were always laughing. I can't remember any sad times at all.

My father was the big one. Big in body and big in spirit. As a kid, I never had any bother about believing in giants. I had my own giant. He seems pretty big to me even now; six feet two and as broad as a house. But then . . . He would pick me up and toss me to the ceiling. From when I was a baby 'til I was over twelve. My mother used to fret that he would drop me. But he'd just say, 'Never missed a catch in my life, and he's much more precious than any ball.' Then give his great laugh and toss me up some more.

I loved it. I could never get enough. 'Again,' I would shout, when I was little. ''Gain, 'Gain!' 'Til even my giant father collapsed in a chair, red in the face, and said enough was enough.

It was such a feeling, being thrown in the air, like flying; and those giant hands closing round my waist never missed. I'd have let him hold me out over Niagara Falls, and laughed . . .

Sometimes he'd snatch me up shouting, 'Come and see,' after he'd pulled up at our front door in a screech of brakes and flying gravel. And there would be a new fast open car he'd just bought. His great weakness was cars. Then he would whirl me off, with the wind streaming through my hair, to see some new building he was constructing, all mysterious trenches and scaffolding reaching up into the sky. Or so it seemed to me then. Always making things, my father. I thought he was rebuilding the whole world, so it would soon all be shiny and new and his kingdom.

Sometimes he drank too much, especially when I was small. But even drunk, I was not afraid of him. He could still always catch me when he threw me in the air. And the drink just made him funnier. He was never sick or nasty or anything.

But I remember once he was so drunk after a party

for clients that he couldn't walk when he got home. He just lay on the hearth rug and laughed helplessly while my mother told him he was legless. That worried me; the idea that one day he might have no legs, and seem very small, and not be able to throw me up to the ceiling any more . . .

But he seemed to me most glorious on Saturdays, when my mother took me to watch him play rugby at Rostyn Park. We sat in the old wooden stand, that could put splinters into the backs of your legs if you squirmed about too much. All around were men in cloth caps, who took the smoking pipes from their mouths to shout hoarse encouragement as my father, splendid in blue and white hoops, tree-trunk hairy legs gleaming in the weak winter sun, pounded towards the enemy goal-line with the ball tucked under his arm. And the crowd of opponents clustering around him like flies, leaping on to his back, hanging on there two or three at a time, 'til they fell off again and lay glaring, while my father pounded on, bent almost double.

Oh, how he could twist and turn and wriggle, 'til they finally bore him to the ground by sheer weight of numbers. And I would wait with bated breath for him to emerge from the bottom of a mountain of lesser giants. But always he rose up whole, pushing his lock of dangling hair from his eyes (he had hair in those days) or spitting blood, or even, one terrible day, a tooth. I noted carefully where that tooth fell. And, as the final whistle went, and he came off the field among his mates, steaming like a racehorse in the cold air, I crept out on to the muddy pitch, trampled by a million studded bootmarks, to search for the tooth, the part of him that was lost. I found it, finally, and ran into the changing room with it, among all the muddy, naked giants, very poorly concealed inside towels, who appeared suddenly and then vanished again through the clouds of steam and the sweet smell of embrocation.

I wasn't at all afraid. I was his son.

When I gave him the tooth, he gave the biggest laugh I'd ever heard, and all the other giants laughed too, and he shouted, 'Every hair of my head is numbered.'

They all shouted back, 'You've got a good lad there, Horsie!'

They called him Horsie because I'd first called him that. Sitting on his shoulders, hanging on to that lock of hair, shouting, 'Gee up, Horsie!' as he capered round the room, sending the odd chair crashing over on to its back.

We always lived in big new houses, when I was small. Later (and this was my mother's doing) we lived in an older, half-timbered house, full of pretty

4

little antiques she'd bought. Over the years, she had a soothing effect on my father. When they were first married, he'd build anything, anywhere, and to hell with the look of the countryside. Later, to please her, he took to buying up old buildings, houses and barns, and doing them up so they blended in with their surroundings. And she cared about people, even more than she cared about buildings. She was a county councillor, always on the phone even while she was cooking supper, looking worried, concerned. And there were always desperate people coming to the house without warning and staying for hours. And I would linger outside the lounge door, listening to the rumble of voices and wishing my mum had time to be like other boys' mums, always there if you wanted a chat, and making you a sandwich when you got home from school.

She was little and dark and always laughing then, except when she was helping somebody in trouble, and when you walked down the street with her, everyone seemed to know her and say hello. I don't know how she remembered everybody's names, but she did.

Oh, I felt very *safe* with them. But I suppose I was lonely for somebody my own size, my own age. I invented an imaginary invisible friend called Mr Figgis, who, my mum said, went everywhere with me.

So when my brother came along, I loved him. Right from the start. The moment Andrew, Andy, was born, nobody ever heard of Mr Figgis again. Andy took his place. Except that sometimes, when we were alone, I called *him* 'Figgis'. It was a joke between us.

I was three when he was born. My parents were scared I might be jealous. But how could I be jealous of him? He was *mine*, like Mr Figgis had been. It wasn't just that I tried to help, like fetching Mum a nappy from the drawer. I used to spend hours watching him while he was asleep. Wondering what he would say, once he could talk. Where we would go together, once he could walk. Sometimes it seemed to me he *was* me, because we'd been made by the same Mum and Dad. Sometimes I knew he wasn't me, for he would moan in his sleep, at a time when I felt happy. Or smile in his sleep, when I felt sad. It was awful, that we couldn't talk to each other yet. But I would poke his tiny clenched fist with my finger, where it lay on the blue coverlet. And his hand would open like a flower, then clench hard on my finger, and I would know we were mates, and that he knew it too. Sometimes I would stalk into the kitchen indignantly, if Mum wasn't quick enough in coming, and announce Figgis was crying.

He needed a lot of looking after, did Figgis. He was always a restless sleeper. He would moan or laugh, throw himself about, so you would know he was having a big dream. Sometimes he looked so upset, I would want to wake him out of it. But Mum said that was wrong. He must dream his own dreams, and get them out of his system.

I suppose in a way I was envious of his dreams. All I ever do is snore, when I'm asleep. Or if I do dream, I can never remember them. I used to ask him about his dreams, but he was pretty cagey, always. Sometimes I'd get one out of him, like:

'I dreamt we lived in a castle, and the Queen Mum came to stay, and we all had to act as butlers and servants. And there were lots of trees in pots along our drive. But when the Queen Mum went home, Dad took them all back to the shop.'

But I knew these were just his *little* dreams. I suppose I always wanted more.

Two

Things

What was really strange about Figgis was his Things. He had Things about people, and Things about things. Obsessions, I suppose you'd call them now; but we just said he was having one of his Things.

In the beginning, it would just be some object he had picked up. An ice-lolly stick, or a stone with funny markings. Mum said it was quite usual, this infant curiosity. We should be glad he didn't try to eat coal or soil, like some little kids did.

But Figgis was *so* curious. Who, he demanded, had eaten the lolly and thrown down the stick? Was it a boy or a girl? How old were they? What flavour had the ice lolly been? (Sometimes I could answer that by licking the mucky old stick, and getting a ghost of a taste of orange or raspberry. This would drive Mum mad. But I had to tell the kid *something*. He went on insisting so.)

Or how old was the stone? Where had it come

from? How had it got there? My father, in desperation, even got a book out of the library on geology. But it didn't do him much good. The stones Figgis found were never in the book.

It was worse when Figgis had a Thing about people. Even at two he would let go of your hand and run up to a perfect stranger, and say 'hello' and then just stare at them solemnly, as if searching out their very soul. Of course, old ladies adored it, and he usually ended up getting a sweet or a 20p piece. Dad said he was a crafty, commercially-minded little sod. But it wasn't the sweets or money that Figgis was after. He often gave me the sweets or the money, or just left them lying about.

And it wasn't just old ladies either. It could be a policeman sitting in his Panda, or a filthy babbling tramp, or even a glamorous young lady. The police were pretty good with him, and he seemed to have a way of charming the tramps. It was the glamorous young ladies who found him difficult, though Dad had fun sorting them out, much to Mum's annoyance.

We tried to work out why Figgis was so fascinated by some people and not others. I mean, it wasn't *all* the policemen, or *all* the tramps. Or all the young ladies. Just the odd one, and they weren't any handsomer or happier, or sadder or smellier than the others he ignored. We asked Figgis, but he wouldn't

9

say. Or couldn't. After all, he was only two or three at the time.

The first big Thing occurred when he was about six. The strange case of Charlie Mbajumo . . .

It started with a picture in the *Guardian*. Of an African witch doctor dressed in his full working gear. Carved mask over his face, feathers in his headdress, a necklace of animal teeth round his neck. You know the kind of thing – quite spectacular really. I could understand why the kid was fascinated.

What we couldn't understand was why Figgis insisted the witch doctor was called Charlie Mbajumo. Because the photograph wasn't attached to a newspaper article or anything. It was just a stray photo to fill up a gap in the paper, with the caption, 'A Nigerian witch doctor prepares to exorcise spirits from a sick tribesman during the spring fertility festival.' I mean, all the interest was in the weird gear he was wearing.

But that wasn't enough for Figgis. It wasn't enough for him that Mum cut the photo out for him, and mounted it on a bit of yellow card, and pinned it on the wall by his bed. It wasn't enough that Dad had it enlarged really huge on his drawing-office copier at work, and hung that on the wall as well. Figgis was going to write a letter to Charlie Mbajumo or die in the attempt. He had no other topic of conversation; he went on about it morning noon and night, 'til he drove us all mad.

It was lucky we had pretty smart parents, who knew their way around the world. Dad went after the newspaper and the photographer, and Mum went after the cultural attaché at the Nigerian embassy in London. It took a long time. The photographer only remembered he'd taken the picture in a small village north of Benin. (He'd been in Cambodia and Lebanon since then.) The cultural attaché (and he was very good, or else he didn't have much else to do) told us first that the witch doctor was a member of the Ibo tribe, and then, after several Figgis-ridden agonising weeks, came up with the bloke's name and address.

The staggering thing, for me the truly staggering thing, was that the bloke *was* really called Charlie Mbajumo . . .

Mum and Dad just gave each other a look, and then shrugged their shoulders. Funny how blind even the best adults are. I mean, it was a miracle, a telepathy at ten thousand miles range, but they just shrugged and forgot it. Dad had his next big rugby match to worry about, and the slipshod plumbers at his new Carlton Hotel, and Mum had her council work. But *I* remembered.

And we all helped Figgis write his slow painful letter, on Mum's best notepaper with flowers down

11

the left-hand edge. The letter was nothing special. Figgis just wanted to write, 'Hello, Charlie, how are you? My name is Andy and I live in Britain. Will you write me a letter? Is it hot where you live? Are there lots of big animals? Love, Andy.'

But Mum and Dad said he ought to call him 'Mr Mbajumo'; it was more polite.

I don't think we expected a reply really, but one came. It had pictures of animals on the envelope. There were photos inside. Charlie Mbajumo in his civvies; an Elton John tee-shirt and spotless white jeans and bare feet. Grinning at the camera. He was obviously pretty well off, for he had a five-roomed house, even if the roof was just corrugated iron. And a big shiny old American car he was obviously very proud of. His writing was sprawly but very clear. The letter was full of stories about animals. The only scary thing was that the letter started 'Dear Figgis', whereas we could all have sworn that Figgis had signed his letter 'Andy', and never mentioned Figgis at all. Still, that letter wasn't around any more, so we couldn't check.

Figgis and Charlie exchanged another couple of letters, before Figgis found some other Thing and lost interest.

Three

Squirrel

The baby squirrel wasn't so funny.

We were packing up to go camping in France. We were going to drive through the night and catch the ferry from Dover. Mum had gone into town to do the last-minute shopping, and Dad was busy checking over the camping gear and getting it loaded on to the roof of our Volvo estate.

It was about three o'clock when I heard Figgis yelling for me. He was about seven years old by then. I found him crouched over something on our lawn, which Dad had just mown.

I thought it was a kitten at first. Our cat's had lots of kittens, and I thought this was a week-old kitten, with its ears still flat to its skull, and its bulging eyes still tight shut. It was lying quite motionless in the sunlight on our lawn, but you could see it was still breathing. Its side was going up and down, first slowly, then really fast, as if it was panting.

13

I wondered if the panting meant it was in pain, or dying. I wondered if it was a kitten our she-cat had found and stolen. So when she turned up, I raged at her, for her stupidity at stealing another cat's kitten, then just leaving it.

Then I slowly realised it wasn't a kitten, it was a young squirrel. I wondered if it had fallen out of its nest in one of our trees. I could see that its hindlegs were bent in a very strange unnatural way, and I thought they were broken and my heart despaired. I mean, Mum and Dad were pretty good about helping hurt and stray animals, but what the hell could you do for a week-old squirrel with two broken legs?

But Figgis was looking at me, with those great bottomless eyes of his.

'It's lost,' he said. 'It wants its mother.' Which meant, rescue it, Tom. Make the world all right for it again. Such trust, such faith. I felt sick. I scanned all the trees in our garden. Not a sign of a squirrel, let alone a nest. I never felt so helpless, so utterly helpless in my life. So I yelled for my dad. He came, good-natured as always, but up to his ears in packing. I watched him, and saw the same pain in his face. He nodded his head towards the kitchen door and I followed him, out of earshot of Figgis.

'I think both its back legs are broken,' I whispered.

'The kindest thing would be to kill it. Put it out of

14

its misery.' Then he said, wretchedly, 'I hate killing anything, but it'll have to be done. We can't leave it behind for the cat to torment.'

We looked at Figgis through the kitchen window. He was busy building a little nest for the squirrel, with the green lawn clippings my father's mower had left that morning. A fly kept landing on the squirrel, and he kept waving his hand to shoo it away. Then he took off his sunhat, to shield the squirrel from the sun. As we watched, he turned and saw us, and looked at us accusingly.

'It's hungry,' he shouted. 'It's thirsty. *C'mon.*'

'We can't kill it,' I said. 'He'd go berserk. He'd never trust us again.'

'Can you take him for a walk?' asked my father. 'So I can deal with it? Take him to the shop and buy him some sweets. Then when he comes back, I can say I've put it back into its nest in the prunus tree.'

'He wouldn't believe you. He'd want to see it in its nest. He's not a dim kid any more, you know.' For once, I felt like kicking my father.

'Look, for God's sake, I've got the car to pack,' said my father. He wasn't being callous, he was being desperate; anything to get away from the situation. Though he did have the car to pack, and we didn't have any time to lose. 'Keep an eye on them.' And he went back to the garage and his packing, and for once

I *hated* him. I wasn't any better, mind. I just stood and watched Figgis, making the grassy nest bigger and bigger, and brushing away the fly. I was glad when our cat Minnie came home again, and showed far too much interest in the squirrel, and I was able to get some action chasing her away as fast and as far as I could. It made me feel not quite totally useless . . .

But it was a long, long time, watching Figgis loving the squirrel, mourning over the squirrel, *being* the squirrel. He looked so lonely . . .

And then Mum came home, and damned us for a bunch of helpless males, and sorted us out, as she so often did.

'Of course its back legs aren't broken! Young squirrels' legs always bend back like that. That's how they can climb so well, when they grow up. It must be starving, poor little thing. Go the bathroom, Tom, and get the eye-dropper and wash it *thoroughly*, and warm some milk in the pan, as warm as your hand, no *warmer*. Horsie! Horsie! Stop mucking about in that garage, and look up the number of the RSPCA!'

And there she was, squirrel in one hand, phone in the other, feeding the squirrel and talking to the RSPCA at the same time.

Miraculously, there was a girl at the RSPCA who specialised in young squirrels that had fallen out of

16

the nest. When Dad had finished packing the roof-rack of the car, we all drove up together, with the squirrel in a cardboard box full of shredded writing paper from Mum's special supply, because Figgis was scared newsprint would rub off and poison the squirrel . . .

The girl thought she could cope with the squirrel OK. Figgis gave her a long hard look. Then said, 'I shall come and see it, when we get back from France.'

'It'll be much bigger by that time. It will have its eyes open, and a little bushy tail. They grow awfully quickly.' She smiled; she was nice.

Figgis was not entirely convinced. 'If you're not sure you can manage, I'm not going to France. I'm staying *here*.' He planted his feet extra-firmly, and went on staring at her.

'I've done it lots of times,' said the girl, who had turned a little pale. 'I've raised ones that were far smaller than this. Honest.'

'All right,' said Figgis, a bit happier. A fisherman came in and Figgis saw what he was carrying. Two seabirds black with oil, only their yellow eyes staring out desperately from an oily white plastic carrier bag.

'C'mon,' snapped my father, and literally dragged Figgis out of the door.

We had oil pollution and seabirds all the way to

the channel coast. Nobody got a wink of sleep, that journey.

There *was* a happy ending. When we got back the squirrel was still alive, and cuddled into the girl's shoulder, and looked at us with bright inquisitive eyes.

'What's going to happen to it? When it gets big?' asked Figgis.

'It can stay in my house 'til it's fully grown,' said the girl. 'But then they really start to bite, and I'll have to take it to the little zoo in Walton Park.'

'Not in a *cage*,' said Figgis, ominously. 'It mustn't live in a *cage*.' World War Three was starting to brew up again. 'Why can't you just let it *go*?'

'It wouldn't know how to be a wild squirrel. It wouldn't know how to find nuts, and bury acorns in the ground for the winter. It never had a mother to show it how. It would starve to death. The cage at Walton Park's very big – ten yards long. And it will have branches to climb on, and everyone will feed it with peanuts and biscuits. It'll have a *lovely* time.'

'Make sure nobody gives it chewing gum,' said Figgis darkly. 'Or it'll choke to death.'

And that was that. Except for endless trips to Walton Park to check up on *our* squirrel. I couldn't tell it from its four little mates in the end, but Figgis always reckoned he could. The president of the United States wasn't more carefully watched over than our squirrel. It died at the ripe old age of three, and we brought back the body to bury in our garden.

He could always twist us round his little finger.

Four

Bossa

Not all Figgis's Things were a pain in the neck. There were his great sea dreams, which went on for weeks. The first was all glittering icebergs and kayaks and avalanches of snow falling endlessly into the sea, making great spreading waves. People with furry hoods round their faces, and slant-eyed fat babies done up in tight bundles.

The second, which went on even longer, was a sort of South Sea island fantasy, all ships sailing with outriggers, and people singing and laughing and feasting round bonfires on the beach.

'Wonderful imagination that child's got,' said my mother.

'Just David Attenborough stuff,' said my father. 'You let those kids watch too much telly.'

'You try stopping them,' said my mother. 'They just go next door to the Holmes'. Telly's never off in that house.'

But I wasn't sure it *was* all imagination or telly. Because Figgis assured me these were real people in his dreams, and he never watched that kind of programme on the telly; he didn't *need* to. And what he told me was so detailed. He even showed me some of the knots they used, to tie things together.

I tried catching him out more than once. There were some loose pages in Mum's old encyclopaedias – coloured illustrations of fish of the world. I showed Figgis the page on North Atlantic fish, and asked him if those weren't the fish his South Sea islanders caught? He said of course not, stupid, those were the fish his *Eskimos* caught . . . every time I tried to catch him out, he caught me out. Maybe he just got to those encyclopaedias first; he was a cunning little swine, and a great one for grown-ups' books.

They were fun, Figgis's sea dreams. I enjoyed sharing them with him. His dreams began to seem a natural part of my own life. Only, when you were with him, and he was telling you about them, they seemed, he made them seem, more real than real life. They made real life seem a bit boring, all homework and that . . . But I didn't worry. As I said, they were fun.

Not like the Ethiopian woman and her child. I will never forget the Ethiopian woman. And that kid. They are burnt like blisters on my memory.

We were in Spain at the time; a villa with a maid near Marbella. Figgis would be about ten by then. It was a jolly noisy squabbling time. Mum kept trying to coax us inland off the beach, to explore what she called, 'the real Spain', by which she meant dark, smelly little churches, and old women with no teeth and picturesque donkeys laden with baskets of oranges, just waiting their chance to lash out with their back hooves. Dad kept on driving us up to suss out the new hotels they were building in Marbella, and the new marina, because as a developer he was wondering if there was any money to be made.

Figgis and I just wanted to muck about on the beach.

Squabbling; but happy squabbling. Until the morning Dad bought that copy of the *Observer* with that picture of the Ethiopian woman and her starving kid on the front page. It was just at the start of the worst Ethiopian famine.

I saw Dad coming along the beach, with the folded paper in one hand, and a fistful of ice-creams in the other and I tried to telepathise to him, 'Dad, for God's sake, don't let Figgis see that photo.'

But my father, alas, is not psychic; especially when surrounded by young ladies who have mislaid the top part of their bikinis.

Figgis was. He snatched that newspaper from

22

under Dad's arm before he had a chance to sit down. Then just sat there, staring at the photograph. Wouldn't touch his ice-cream; I had to eat it for him, before it totally melted.

He sat there all morning, just staring at that photograph. A little dark patch of misery among all the sun and lovely girls, and flashing-eyed Spanish blokes throwing Frisbees to show off their muscles to the stray English birds. He created a hole in the landscape, a black hole, that made the white hotels and the crashing waves, even the blue sky, seem like a badly-painted backdrop to a third-rate play. Even to me, as time went on, none of the stuff around me was real; only the gaunt dignified woman and her swollen-bellied, huge-eyed brat. They filled the world.

People around us began to notice. Figgis was so still, so utterly cut off from us. A thin, bald man with a bank-manager moustache, over-pink bare chest and ridiculous red Bermuda shorts came across and said to my father, 'Your son OK? He's not got sunstroke, has he?'

'He's OK,' said my father, and I could tell from the bitten-off way he said it that he was very very angry. My father hates any kind of scene in public . . .

Shortly afterwards, the bank manager's whole family got up and walked off down the beach, with all their stuff. I wondered if it was just coincidence, but

23

then another family got up and moved away as well. There was an empty space forming round us, an area of blank sand on what was a pretty crowded beach. A new family moved into the space, but after half an hour of Figgis, they, too, moved out. We were becoming isolated, shut out, and my father hates that.

He made a sudden move towards Figgis. My mother said, 'Don't,' which checked him for a moment. And then my father snatched the newspaper from Figgis's hands, and tore it slowly and terribly into tiny strips.

Figgis got to his feet, gave him one stark look, and then walked away into the crowd.

'Don't worry,' said my father. 'He'll be back in a minute.'

How little he knew Figgis. Figgis was gone for nearly an hour. Mum got frantic, and went to look for him.

And then Figgis came back. With another copy of the *Observer*. And settled on the sand with that awful photograph exactly as before. Where had he scrounged it? English papers were rare out there, then. *Observers* anyway.

He really had Dad going now. Dad's huge hand was clawing into the sand, like an excavator shovel. Digging a great big hole and throwing the sand any old where. The veins were standing out on his balding brow. I knew there was going to be a terrible explosion.

So did Mum. She marched Figgis up the beach with a hand on his thin arm, clenched so tight I thought she was going to snap it in half.

Dad looked at me. His rage was already clouding over with shame, because he loved Figgis. But I have never seen him so angry in all my life. I had to help him, or he might have had a heart attack or something. And I loved him as I loved nobody else in the world; because we are so alike, him and I. I knew exactly how he felt. It would have done him good to explode into action, score ten tries on the rugger field and tear the opposing scrum in half. But all he had was me.

'He went too far,' I said. 'We spoil him. He gets far too much attention, with his silly games . . .'

'I bust my guts out,' said my father. 'I work every hour that God sends, to give us a decent life. It's not funny, you know. I was nearly bankrupt twice last year, Tom, thanks to slow payers . . . and all he can think of to do is to ruin the one decent holiday I get in a year . . .'

'He's upset about the Ethiopians starving . . .' I said, gently. It was very hard to be on both their sides at once.

'Ethiopians, Bangladeshis, earthquake victims,

Sudanese. There's no end to them, Tom. You could give every penny you had, and it would just be swallowed up and make not a ha'porth of difference. You could strip yourself naked, and there'd still be more of them, only you'd be in the bread queue yourself by then. A man's entitled to see something for all the work he's put in . . . good God, I'm in Rotary . . . we do a lot to help old people and disadvantaged kids. Charity begins at home . . .'

'I'm on your side,' I said. 'They breed like rabbits, and then they can't feed themselves. If they were birds or foxes dying, people would just call it the balance of nature. Two-thirds of the birds and foxes born every year die of starvation. But when it's people . . . any *people* . . .'

'Steady on, Tom. I can't be *that* ruthless. We must do what we can for them.' He was calming down now, which was my intention. I'm not really all that ruthless either. But Dad's a decent guy, and I didn't like seeing him hurt.

'Do you think,' asked Dad, staring down the beach, 'if I gave Figgis some pesetas, and we could find the right charity to give them to, that that would snap him out of it?'

'Might help,' I said, though I thought it wouldn't be that easy. 'I don't know if the Spanish have charities. I mean, you never hear of the Spaniards doing anything to help internationally. Maybe they're not a charitable nation. All them awful bullfights . . .'

'Heck, don't mention bullfights in front of Figgis. I don't think he's caught on to them yet . . .' My father laughed, creakily. But laughed. I was glad to see it. Then he said, thoughtfully, 'I suppose we could try the bank. Barclays at home sometimes collects money for charities – the big appeals.'

'It's gone one o'clock,' I said. 'The banks will all be shut.'

'We'll go first thing tomorrow . . .'

'Tomorrow's Saturday . . .'

'Oh, no,' said my father. 'The whole weekend. I shall go out of my tiny shiny mind . . .'

'So will I,' I said. And we grinned at each other wryly, and it was OK between us.

Just as well. Because Figgis continued to be a total pain. He wouldn't eat dinner at all that night. He still had his light on at three o'clock in the morning, looking at that picture.

'Hell's sake, Figgis,' I yelled at him. 'Don't you know what time it is? There's *some* of us like to sleep. It's like sharing a room with a nutcase.' I was hoping to provoke him into a row, get him out of it.

But he only said, 'His name is Bossa. He's very hungry. His insides hurt. He can't understand why his mother won't give him food.'

'Suit yourself, nutcase,' I yelled, rolled over and pulled the sheet over my face and went to sleep.

First thing I saw in the morning was Figgis still looking at the photograph. I don't think he'd moved at all, all night. It was really creepy.

He wouldn't eat any breakfast, or any lunch. Dad was all for taking him to the English doctor, giving him a jab of something to cure him. But good old Mum just said, 'Leave him to me. You and Tom go off and do something.'

We did. We went off and hired one of those pedalos, those boats where you sit side by side and move by pedalling. Have you ever seen a pedalo moving as fast as a power boat? You should have seen us, that afternoon. We really worked off our feelings on our poor legs. I could hardly walk when we got off. But it did us good. Then Dad took me into a bar, and bought me a San Miguel; it was the first beer I ever drank in my life, and it was great. I had another one, and Dad had a lot. We were a bit wobbly, finally going home in the car.

When we got there, we found Mum in our bedroom with Figgis.

'You and Tom sleep together tonight, Horsie. I'll cope in here.'

Well, out of sight, out of mind. The maid had gone off duty, and Dad and I had a big fry-up, and to hell with the heat. I suppose it was a silent mutual protest against Figgis starving himself.

And that was the way it went, until nine on the Monday morning, when the doors of Barclays in Marbella swung open. Dad drew out a hundred quids' worth of pesetas, God bless him, and then we had a right hoo-hah with the staff, who were all Spanish in spite of it being Barclays, and who didn't know Oxfam from Oxo cubes.

Eventually Dad established that they *had* heard of the International Red Cross, and Figgis solemnly counted the notes into the sympathetic lady's hand, and she gave him a big receipt marked, 'Ethiopian Appeal Fund. For Bossa.'

I don't think it fooled Figgis for a moment, but Mum must have worked very hard on him, because he played his part in the game without a protest. He was pretty weary by that time, and pretty pale, and he'd lost weight, you could see it in his bare arms and legs. He just seemed anaesthetised, half-asleep.

We were walking down the beach, feeling a little better, but not much, when Figgis suddenly stopped stock-still and said: 'Bossa's dead.'

And I thought oh God, what *now*?

But he only said in a very matter of fact way, 'Can I have an ice-cream?' and my dad positively *ran* to get him one.

Afterwards, he slept in the shade of our beach umbrella nearly all day, and wakened up ravenously hungry. And that was that. We watched him like a hawk for several more days, but he acted perfectly normal, and just went back to searching the beach for funny stones and shells, and we never heard about Bossa again. In the end, it was a great holiday.

So there we were. Until last year, we'd still have called ourselves a typical ordinary English family. I mean, you may think by this time that Figgis was pretty odd, because I've told you all about his peculiar times. But you must remember there were long gaps in between when he was just an ordinary, happy-go-lucky kid. And everybody's brother's odd in some way; either they're crazy about train spotting, or can bend their tongue double-jointed into a horseshoe shape, or spend hours standing on their heads or something.

Dad was past his best at rugby by then. His great county days were over, and he had the start of a beer paunch and was nearly as bald as a coot. But he still played for the second fifteen, and Mum and Figgis and I still went along every week to cheer him on, as he scored his cunning little tries. And I was playing for the under-fifteens at school, and Dad came to watch me on Saturday mornings, returning the compliment. And he said I had the makings of a decent little scrum half.

And Mum was getting a lot more influence on the county council, to help her deserving cases. Everything was hunky-dory.

And then it happened.

I was nearly fifteen by then, and Figgis was twelve.

Five

Gulf

It started that August; the fourth, I think. We'd rented a stone farmhouse in North Wales. There was a paddock behind, that sloped down to the river, where Figgis and I camped out in our tent. I mean, we had a bedroom in the house, next to Mum and Dad's at the front. But who wants to snore away indoors in warm dry weather, when you can fall asleep to the sound of wind and rustling leaves and wake up in the dawn, to the sound of all the birds singing?

It was just after dawn, that first morning. I wakened up with a jump, because somebody further up the paddock was yelling out. In what seemed to me, in my fuddled state, to be a sort of wild triumph.

And I realised, when I started to listen properly, that they were yelling out in a foreign language too. A weird, harsh language, not French or German or Spanish; or even Welsh.

'Hey, Figgis,' I whispered. 'There's some nutcase yelling up by the house.'

He didn't reply. I blindly reached for his shoulder and my hand met an empty sleeping bag. That got me up in a heck of a rush. I didn't feel like facing a nutcase alone and near-starkers.

And besides, Figgis had been known to walk in his sleep.

A weird sight met my eyes, as I staggered out in my shorts. Dad's Volvo was parked up behind the house, silhouetted against the pink dawn. And on top of it a smallish figure sat, leaning forward eagerly and brandishing a big lump of crooked tree branch.

It was, of course, Figgis.

'Come down, you crazy bastard,' I shouted. 'You'll wake up the whole neighbourhood.'

He took not the blindest bit of notice. Didn't even glance in my direction. Just went on leaning forward and brandishing his branch, almost as if the car was a horse and he was urging it forward, to go faster and faster; and shouting in that weird language.

I think I still thought he was taking the mickey out of me even when I got up there. 'Til I saw his face.

It was his features all right. But it was, somehow, not his face. I mean, it was convulsed. Fanatical. Creased up with his yelling. I'll tell you what he

33

looked like. Like the guy who's just scored a goal, in a big FA cup game; the guy who leaps in the air and punches with one fist, before everybody else jumps on to his back and starts thumping him. And he was screaming with triumph like the crowd do when a goal is scored. Only it went on and on and on. Until I began to get really scared. I mean, I knew he was dreaming and sleepwalking and yelling in his sleep. But where was this foreign language coming from? The hairs stood up on the back of my neck, and it wasn't just the morning chill. I knew I shouldn't touch him, or wake him before the dream was over. But the veins were standing out on *his* forehead now; he was wearing himself out. He'd never done anything like this before.

In the end, I did the stupid thing because I couldn't bear to watch it any more. I reached up and grabbed him. He fought like a wild thing. He hit out at me with that branch, and it really hurt. Drew blood, actually. That made me mad, and I threw him down and pinned him to the ground, sitting on his chest, and holding his wrists.

He spat in my face; he tried to bite my hand.

Then finally he lay still, and just glared at me. I thought it was over, then. But it wasn't. It still wasn't Figgis's face. It was full of rage and hate, and at the same time, scared and shifty. Like he hated

34

me, and yet was afraid of me. His eyes looked all hot and dark.

And then he came out of it, and it was Figgis again, looking up at me all puzzled.

'Tom? What's going on? Get off me chest. You're heavy.'

I rolled off and lay there looking at him sideways, along the ground, through the longish grass.

'You were having a dream. *Some* dream . . .'

'There was a desert,' he said. 'All pink and mauve in the sunrise. We were driving very fast. In a lorry. There were lots of us. We knew we were going to win.'

'Who's *we*?'

'Haven't a clue.' He got up and dusted himself down and pulled up his white shorts, which were slipping. 'I'm hungry. Let's go and grab some grub.'

It was while we were in that strange kitchen, ferreting around for all the things you can't find in a strange kitchen, that I turned Mum's radio on.

And got the news that the Iraqis had invaded Kuwait.

'Bloody Saddam,' said my father. 'What's there to stop him? His army could go down the Gulf coast like a dose of salts. He could be sitting in Riyadh in a week. Sitting on half the world's oil. There's nothing even the Americans could do, once he got there. The Saudis have got nowt to stop him with. He's got us by the short and curlies . . .'

'Eat your breakfast, dear,' said my mother. 'I'm sure there are better minds than yours working on it. Will it send the price of petrol up again?'

'Up and up and up,' said my father. 'He'll be able to charge us what he likes. And spend the money on arms against Israel. It's worse than 1940. That fat-gutted bastard holding the world to ransom. It's not to be borne . . .' He leapt up, as if he was going to deal with it there and then.

'Finish your breakfast,' said my mother. 'Then you can go down to the garage, before the price goes up.'

'But,' said my father. 'But . . .'

'Are we going to Bala Lake today, Dad?' asked Figgis, who was lost in a book on bird-watching. 'We might see a red kite. It says they're spreading out that way.'

He wasn't a warlike character, our Figgis. Never.

It wasn't one of our best holidays ever. Dad was no fun at all, with his ear permanently stuck in the car radio 'til Mum threatened divorce if the name Saddam Hussein was mentioned again.

But there was no more bother from Figgis; except that sometimes I'd come half out of sleep and think I heard him mumbling that strange harsh language again. But I never wakened up enough to be sure.

Six

Hair

We had no more trouble 'til the beginning of September; time for us to go back to Elmborough Grammar. Elmborough's fee-paying, all blazers and white shirts and school ties; and the head, Rook the Crook, is fussy about haircuts.

I went down to our usual barber's, Fred Tomlinson's. Fred's well-thought-of at Elmborough Grammar, amongst the lads, because he knows what you can get away with, in haircuts, down to the last millimetre. From twenty years' experience, he can sort of read Rook the Crook's mind, term by term. He keeps us legal, yet fashionable, and he makes a fortune at it.

When he had finished that last little bit of snipping at the back of my neck, and held up his mirror for my approval he said, 'Your Andy not with you?'

'He hadn't finished his breakfast. He was going to follow me down. I don't know where he's got to.'

'Hope he hasn't taken his custom *elsewhere*,' said Fred with a menacing sniff. 'They'll do anything down *that* place. The Head's always sending them back to me, afterwards. Sheer waste of money going down there . . .' He flicked off loose hairs from the back of my neck and gave me a clean cloth to wipe my face with.

I thought I'd nip down to the other place, just in case. Younger brothers do get funny ideas, sometimes. I wanted to head off trouble at home, if I could; and Figgis's not turning up at Fred's wasn't like him at all.

It was as well I did. Because I'd no sooner got there, and begun peering through the cards showing Mohicans and all kinds of perversities, when this kid comes walking out. It was the clothes I recognised first. His 'Friends of the Earth' sweatshirt and those jeans he tie-dyed himself. I'd never have recognised his face. It was all bone and nose and big dark eyes. Because his skull was shining through what looked like a faint dark mist.

He'd had every bit of it off. Like a convict, in some old book. Like skinheads used to be.

Like a soldier.

'For God's sake,' I said. 'What the hell have you done that for? It's not even *fashionable*. They'll *crucify* you at school.'

'To keep the lice off,' he said, without thinking.

39

'*What* lice? What do you mean, lice? We don't have lice in Elmborough. I've never *heard* of anybody having lice.'

'I don't know what lice, Tom,' he said. And his lips trembled. If he hadn't been twelve, I think he would have cried. He suddenly looked terribly young and terribly scared. And a bit like a concentration-camp victim.

'You'll have to stay off school,' I said. 'Pretend you're ill. Even I can't defend you with hair like that.'

'How long will it take to grow?' he whispered.

'You'll still look like a lavatory brush in three weeks' time. I suppose you could say then that you're imitating that Yank who comes on telly to tell us what Uncle Norman Schwarzkopf's thinking . . . you might get away with it.'

I won't go into what Mum said. Or the considerably louder and more that Dad said. But they listened to me and kept him off school for two weeks. I think they just couldn't face up to what Rook the Crook would say. They sent a note saying he'd sprained his ankle, and Figgis was such a law-abiding character, never in trouble, that they got away with it. I had to hump all his schoolwork home for him. When he finally got back to school he was teased a bit, but not much. In fact one or two of his more stupid contemporaries went in for the same haircut, thinking it was with-it to imitate the US marines.

Rook the Crook wasn't pleased, I can tell you.

It was nearly half term before the next Thing happened, and then it didn't scare me much, because it was quiet.

Figgis began singing little strange contented songs in his sleep. They certainly weren't pop songs, nor even acid rock or heavy metal. They just went on and on, rhythmically up and down and rather shapeless. I mean, you'd just have thought he was making them up. The only funny thing about them was that they did go on and on, almost as if he didn't bother taking any breaths. And then, one night, when I'd got quite used to sleeping happily through them, I came wide awake for some reason.

He was sitting on his bed with his legs crossed under him, and he was waggling one hand in front of him, almost as if he was stirring a pot of something.

But the really weird thing was that, in his other hand, he held our communal air rifle. He was sort of leaning his chin against it, as he stirred away with his other empty hand.

The oddest thing was, he'd lost interest in that air rifle months ago. He'd never been really keen, because he loved birds and animals so much, and he knew very well what kids with air rifles did to birds and animals. As I said, he'd shot a few targets with me, and then lost interest. Now I shot targets by myself . . .

But he looked so at home with his gun and his stirring-gestures that it somehow made me nosy. So, very quietly, so as not to wake him, I went across and sat down next to him.

He turned and looked at me, and murmured something in that funny language. His eyes had that look again. Quick, street-wise, restless, curiously hot. Arrogant and yet uneasy. Not like his ordinary straight look at all.

I began to try to sing along with his song. I knew his new songs pretty well by that time. We sang along softly together. And things began to sort of filter through to me. He felt as if he was in some sort of camp; that he was . . . cooking something to eat. It was weird, just sitting there, singing. And then I did another pretty stupid thing, almost without thinking. One of the songs sounded a bit like a line out of 'Heartbreak Hotel', the old Elvis number, and something made me make it *more* like 'Heartbreak Hotel'. And then, a bit cruelly, I began to sing 'Heartbreak Hotel' itself. He gave me one hot-eyed suspicious look, and then I saw he was starting to come out of it.

Finally, he said, 'Tom?' in a puzzled voice.

'Yeah. Where you been, kid?'

'We fill an old can with sand, and then pour petrol on the sand, and light it, to warm the rice.'

'Where are you, Figgis?'

'I don't know,' he said. Then, 'In my bedroom.'

And that was all I could get out of him.

Seven

Victory

The rest of that term, up 'til Christmas, was a good one for our family. The chairman of the council's social services committee resigned in a huff, and they made Mum the new chairperson. We had our school concert and Figgis, who was brilliant on the piano, played two waltzes by Chopin and got a big round of applause.

Mind you, he didn't bring the house down like me and Tosher Briggs and Artie Sumner. We got dressed up in American sailor costume and did, 'There Is Nothing Like A Dame', from *South Pacific*, and all the parents went wild. We had to do three encores, somersaults and handstands and all – we were totally shattered. Parents are always looking for something new to be nostalgic about!

That was the time when I finally got to play rugby in the same team as Dad. Something I'd often done in my daydreams but never in real life. I think it was the thing I wanted most in the world, but I never thought I'd do it. I was getting bigger and stronger all the time, but sadly Dad was getting older, slower and fatter. I knew he'd pack it in, long before I caught up with him.

But that day, Mum and Figgis and I were in the stand, when Dad came out in his rugby gear, with an old bloke in a trilby hat and ancient college scarf and shabby grey overcoat, who I knew ran the second fifteen. I think his name was Wilbraham, Mr Wilbraham. And they stood on the edge of the pitch, glancing across at me every so often, and muttering to each other with increasing vigour. A wild crazy sort of hope ran up me, from my stomach to my head. A feeling I was being . . . considered for something. Finally, I heard Dad say, 'I'll keep an eye on him, Wilbraham, I promise you.' And the old bloke nodded, very reluctantly, and Dad came across and said, 'Go and get your kit. You're playing. Our scrum half's hurt his wrist doing handstands in the changing room. Silly young idiot.'

Mum drove me home; and I got changed in about five seconds, and then ran straight on to the pitch, where they were waiting to start. Dad tossed me a team strip, which I put on over my school strip, to keep me warm and stop me shivering. Though I don't think I was shivering with cold. It was just the unbelievableness of it all. Higgins and Higgins at last! The old firm!

I won't give you a lecture on the game of rugby. Suffice to say that each team has a gang of huge muddy sweating giants called the scrum, who maul and wrestle each other about something cruel, trying to get the ball off each other. And each team also has a row of slim, fast blokes, called the backs, who run with the ball once it's been got, and pass it along their line heading for the opposition goal-line like fiends out of hell.

And the poor soul who joins the two halves of the team together is the scrum half, which was me. He has to scrabble in the mud, among the straining legs of his own giants, and throw the ball out far and fast; before the other team's giants land on top of him like a human avalanche. It's not a lot of fun, when you weigh less than ten stone, to vanish under a hundred and twenty stone of sweating bone and muscle, which is nearly three-quarters of a ton. Not to mention somebody stamping on your outstretched hand with a studded boot . . .

So you will understand I was nervous. But I had Dad at the back of our scrum to help me. What comfort there was in those hairy legs like tree trunks, and that bent-double backside like a horse in black shorts. Old and crafty was my dad, swinging sideways at the back of the scrum, blocking their way as they came to get me, with his large bum or a stuck-out leg, all innocent-like.

So, the first four times I got the ball clear away, with a slight spin on it to steady it through the air, right smack into our stand-off's hands. He began to trust me, and our backs really began to run, and, on the fourth occasion, they scored a try.

This did not suit the enemy scrum half. He was much bigger than me, and nasty with it. An old bloke in his thirties, with a pock-marked face and a wicked little moustache; another ex-county player on his way down, but not cheerful about it, like Dad. The way he used his elbows on me, you'd have thought he'd got six arms, like the goddess Kali. I got the ball away each time, well before he hit me. But he still went on hitting me with his elbow, in my ribs where it hurt most. And it was starting to make me nervous, and my passing was starting to go off. And the referee as usual saw nothing to blow his whistle about . . .

Then Dad wiped some mud off his face, while they were lining up for a line-out, and said to the enemy scrum half, 'Leave the kid *alone.*'

'Get lost,' said the enemy scrum half.

What Dad did then was illegal, unprovable and quite beautiful. He caught the ball in that line-out,

47

and ran straight into the enemy scrum half, instead of trying to dodge round him. He hit him, he knocked him flat, and then he ran up the length of him, as if he was a red carpet. Then he tripped at the last moment, and landed on top of his head. With both knees.

The enemy scrum half just lay there, spitting blood and curses at Dad. They had to have the trainer on, to administer first aid. When the scrum half finally got to his feet, he complained to the referee . . .

'He just got in my way,' said Dad, his face a study in muddy uncomprehending innocence. 'I think he was trying to tackle me, and it went wrong . . .'

The referee walked away in the end.

'You . . .' snarled the scrum half.

'Leave the kid alone. I'm warning you,' said Dad. 'Or you won't be at work on Monday.'

He left me alone after that. I had a good game, though I didn't try anything fancy; just got the ball out clean to the stand-off every chance I had. The scores were level at half-time; Dad and I sucked our oranges together in mutual muddy harmony. He told me I wasn't doing badly, which made me glow from head to foot.

In the second half, he scored two of his specials. The trouble was, the opposition scored twice as well. And converted both to goals, with superb kicks. We were four points behind now, and it was almost time for the whistle to go, and I was shattered.

We were forty yards from their line when the ball came to me out of the heaving mass of legs for the last time.

As I picked it up, Dad yelled, 'Go yourself.'

I looked and saw a great gap in front of me. I had passed the ball straight out so often, the opposition thought I couldn't do anything else. They were already streaming across the field after our backs. There was no one left to stop me . . .

I ran with every ounce of strength left in my failing legs. I made twenty yards before I heard them closing up on me from behind, the thudding boots, the panting. I daren't look round. Their hands grasped for me, caught me. I was falling . . .

And then a great arm closed round me, and . . . it seemed to pick me up. I felt I was flying, flying for that little faint white line on the muddy grass that means so much, and which was just coming into my vision, below my sweaty, flogging hair. My legs were still working away somewhere, but all I could hear was a kind of panting Anglo-Saxon war chant in my ear. It was, it could only be, my father, the great, the incomparable Horsie Higgins, closer to me than my own skin. I could feel his warmth through our two shirts, I could smell his great warhorse sweat. The hands, so many hands, grasping for us. But we didn't stop, although there was someone else pretty heavy hanging round my neck by that time, trying to flatten me.

Now we were both falling, or rather diving. But it was time to fall. The line was right beneath our teetering feet.

We went down with a bang; the ball, beneath me, knocked every ounce of wind out of my straining lungs. I was choking to death, there was a mountain, a cursing sweating mountain lying on my head.

But in the end, it dissolved, and the referee inspected me and the ball, and raised his hand high in the air, and blew his whistle. There were small sounds of cheering, far away in the stand.

We'd scored. My father pulled me to my feet, inspected me up and down, and said, 'You'll live!' Then he said, 'You *scored*,' as if it was all my doing, and he couldn't believe it.

We walked back to the halfway line, his arm round me and all our team throwing playful though painful punches at us.

'Leave off,' said Dad. 'He's too young to die.'

The score was equal, now. We watched in silence while our lanky fullback fiddled about with the ball and a bucket of sand, like fullbacks do, to create their own little bit of drama. Then he did what he was paid to do, and kicked the goal, and we'd won, and then the whistle went.

They nearly mauled us to death in the changing room. They threw muddy boots at us, hit us with wet towels, and did all those other things middle-aged rugby players do to show they love you. But the great cry was, 'Higgins and Higgins – the old firm!'

And just for an hour I shared my father's truest and happiest world, amidst the alternately scalding and freezing showers, and the singing of vile old songs and the comical, obscene, naked dancing. Showers after the match is the one place the middle-aged, middle-class Englishman is really free; if he's won the match. Neither a Roman orgy nor an African tribal dance will ever equal it for laughs . . .

We finally caught up with Mum and Figgis in the tea room, when our everyday clothes had finally restored respectability.

'Well done, Tom!' said Mum, hugging me; and for once I didn't mind being hugged in public.

'Well done, Tom!' said Figgis shyly, admiring for once, and smiled.

We drove back relaxed and happy. Got a crime video and a takeaway curry on the way home.

I think it was our last happy day.

Eight

Tears

Underneath, things were moving. I mean, in Figgis's dream-life. Almost every night now, I'd waken about four, and he'd be sitting on his bed, muttering in that strange dream language. And I got into the habit of getting up and sitting next to him. And I made a discovery.

You couldn't get anything out of him while he was deep in the dream, talking the strange language. And you couldn't get much out of him once he'd wakened up properly. He was just Figgis, with a few vague memories of carrying heavy wooden boxes or eating rice out of a tin with a wire handle.

But there was an in-between stage, when he was just starting to come out of it. And then he still seemed to be somebody else, but understanding and talking English.

'What's your name?' I asked him once, as the hot, flushed, shifty-eyed face turned towards me.

He said something that sounded like 'Latif'.

After that I could sort of summon him out of the dream by calling, 'Latif! Latif!' Then I'd get some really hairy stuff out of him. He said he lived in a place called Tikrit, and his father repaired cars for a living. 'German cars are good,' he said. 'And Russian cars. Yankee cars are rubbish. My father says.'

And he spat on our bedroom carpet. I sat there staring at the little bubbly bit of spit, soaking into the pile. I'd never seen anyone spit before: except into a hanky when they had a cold.

I looked up Tikrit in our atlas; it was north of Baghdad. Then I read in the paper it was where Saddam Hussein himself came from.

But that didn't prove anything. I mean, if I could look it up in the atlas, or the newspaper, so could Figgis. I mean, at that stage, I still reckoned he was making it all up. Another typical Figgis-game. I couldn't be *sure* he wasn't having me on deliberately. Another deep Figgis-joke . . . How wrong I was . . .

But I enjoyed the performance; he could always give a good performance, could Figgis. What an imagination he had!

I would ask him about Saddam Hussein.

'He is our hero. He is not afraid of the Americans. He is the only Arab who is not afraid of the

Americans. The Americans will not bribe him into silence. He will make fools of them, by the force of his will!'

But I learnt to keep off the topic of Saddam in the end. One night he got so worked up he leapt to his feet and began yelling, 'Saddam, Saddam, Saddam!' so loud it brought my mother through in her dressing gown, before I could get him out of the dream.

He wakened up when she spoke to him; looking all dazed and lost as usual. She talked to him softly, in a way that made me feel a bit jealous. Cuddled him, then got him back to bed. Then she turned on me. 'I want a word with you, Tom!'

We sat down in the cold kitchen. The central heating was off, and I began feeling a bit sorry for myself, and wanting to get back to bed.

'Look, Mum, he was only having a bad dream. You know what Andy is. He's always had them.'

Her eyes were too sharp for my liking. 'How often is this happening?'

I shrugged and lied, because I wanted to get back to bed. 'Once or twice.'

'Why didn't you tell me?'

I just shrugged.

'I heard what he was shouting. Is he worried that there's going to be a war?'

'No more than anybody else.'

'A lot of kids are having nightmares about the war. I was talking to Nancy Tarbet in Sainsbury's. Her two are having nightmares. About being burnt alive!'

'They're just little kids. Andy's twelve . . .'

'So that makes him a big tough-guy, I suppose! Like you and your father! You know how Andy *feels* things . . .'

'What do you think Dad and I are? The Magnificent Hulks? Hairy apes?'

'Well, you're not losing much sleep over it, either of you!'

I shrugged again.

'It's all that telly,' she said viciously. 'They have nothing new to say. But they go on saying it. Night after night after night, 'til you could scream. And your father has to listen to every single word. He seems to have forgotten where the "off" switch is.'

I could've said something sharp then. I won't hear a word against my dad. But I just said, 'Are we going to sit here all night? I've got school tomorrow.'

'*Goodnight*!' she said, and stalked out, putting the lights out as she passed the switch, and leaving me to find my way to bed in the dark.

She's not normally spiteful. It came as a shock to me, just how upset she must be.

It was unfortunate that Dad insisted on having the kitchen telly on for the six o'clock news, during supper the following night. I mean, it *was* dead boring. There was nothing new; just that the Americans were pouring in more and more stuff; with the same old video recordings of orange tanks moving through pink dust clouds into a mauve sunset.

'I'm switching this rubbish off!' said Mum.

'No,' said Dad. 'I want it. I want to know what's going to happen.'

'You know damn well what's going to happen,' snapped Mum. 'A lot of people are going to get killed. Because the world is run by *men*! Mrs Simpson's lad's out there. I had her in tears this morning, in the post office.'

'I know what they're going to call this,' said Dad. 'The crying war. Remember when those two Aussie frigates sailed for the Gulf? It wasn't just the sailors' wives crying. It was the flippin' sailors as well. The whole world's gone soft. As for that Gulf Mums' Association, going on about our lads being homesick . . . it's enough to make you weep. How do you think our parents coped in World War II? When my father went to Korea, my mother didn't twitch a muscle. Or she cried in *private*.'

'So we do nothing? And let our lads get killed for *nothing*?'

'It's not nothing. Saddam's nearly got the atomic bomb. Better to lose ten thousand now than a million later.'

'*Ten thousand*?' My mother was nearly screaming. 'You're very free with your ten thousand. When you nearly broke your heart over that baby squirrel on the lawn. I think you're stark raving mad, Horsie. All you men have taken leave of your senses. Suppose it was you who had to go? Or Tom?'

My father's face went as still as a stone. 'I hope I would do my duty,' he said coldly. 'Are you calling me a coward?'

'And I hope I would do my duty as well,' I added, moving about a quarter of an inch closer to Dad.

'Men,' said Mum. But she flushed crimson. She knew she'd gone too far.

'Anyway,' said Dad, in a softer, making-it-up sort of tone. 'It won't be our lads that'll get killed. We'll bomb them to bits before we send our lads in. That Schwarzkopf knows what he's doing.'

'Bomb them to bits?' Mum went up like a rocket again. 'Don't you think the Iraqi soldiers have mothers as well? Or do you think they're made out of metal, like Daleks?'

I looked across at Figgis, who hadn't said a word. He was just staring at film of apricot-coloured Tornados taking off, leaving clouds of puce smoke. I couldn't read the look on his face at all.

Nightgame

I don't know why I pushed Figgis so hard, with that night-time game of ours. I suppose in a way, I'd always envied him. Figgis the dreamer, lost in a world of his own. Figgis, who was never bored with his own company, his own thoughts. Me, I need my mates. If I'm left alone for an evening, I stuff myself with grub from the fridge, I stuff my head with rubbish from the telly, and end up going to bed in a right bad mood. I've got to have things happening; got to have some action.

I suppose this Latif Thing was like a new toy. And I made the most of it, night after night. *Was* Figgis just making it up? If so, I wanted to push him to the far end of it, to catch him out in something stupid that I *knew* was wrong. I'd read a lot about the coming war myself by that time – everything I could lay my hands on.

But whereas I was reading about big military

stuff – bunkers and sand berms and oil-filled ditches waiting to be set alight, I never got that kind of stuff from the Latif character. He went on about playing football, 'til the old ball burst and they couldn't repair it. About the little creatures of the desert; and how the men caught and ate them, because they never had enough to eat. About having his mess-tins stolen, and being in trouble with the major; until his mate Akbar, who was a shepherd and could move silently, stole some new ones for him, from the new crowd further along the line.

And about never getting letters from his mum. And those lice again. He was always trying to get rid of lice; either with a bar of wet soap, or by running a match along the seams of his uniform. Only one thing worried him more than lice. A different major, who had a taste for young boys, if he could corner them alone . . .

Cunning stuff – or was it *true*? I could never make my mind up. It was middle-of-the-night stuff, and the rules are different, somehow, in the middle of the night.

So I didn't notice for a long time that the Latif character was getting stronger and stronger; and I was getting more and more caught up with him.

Until one day in school, I fell fast asleep in the middle of a history lesson. I jolted awake and the teacher and all my mates were laughing at me. I remember the history master, who was a nice bloke called Giddings who I liked, quoted a verse at me:

> 'My candle burns at both ends;
> It will not last the night;
> But ah, my foes, and oh, my friends –
> It gives a lovely light.'

It should have been a warning to me. But I just told myself the history room had been overwarm – it was nearly Christmas by then, and the school boilers were working full out. And all my mates asked if I'd been up half the night boozing at some party, or getting off with some girl. So I didn't take it seriously.

I didn't even take it seriously when Figgis came home with the worst school report he'd ever had. He'd dropped from first to tenth in the end-of-term exams. Mind you, tenth in the top stream at Elmborough Grammar School was still pretty good. But it wasn't Figgis.

Mum went on at him, and then Dad came home and went on at him, then they both went on at him over supper. Oh, they were very liberal, very understanding. Was he worried about something? Was he being bullied? That sort of enlightened parents' crap.

Figgis didn't seem worried, somehow.

And that should have been the biggest warning of all.

That, and the scratching. He developed this terrible habit of scratching. His hair, his armpits, all over. But especially his hair and his armpits. Even when we had people in over Christmas . . . Mum nagged him cruel, made him have baths, even took him to the doctor. The doctor found lots of raw red marks all over him, the results of the scratching. But no *reason* for the scratching. He booked him in to have tests done by some sort of skin specialist, after the New Year.

Figgis never got to have those tests.

Ten

Hospital

The day before the start of school in January, I escorted Figgis down to the barber's personally. I wasn't having that nonsense happen again. And it didn't.

But he fell asleep in the barber's chair. I didn't notice at first, because, waiting to have mine cut, I was deep in a new motoring magazine, wondering what I could persuade Dad to buy me, once I passed my test. It wasn't until he began talking that strange guttural language that I dropped the magazine and stared in horror. Everybody else in the shop was staring too, Fred standing like a frozen statue with his long thin comb in one hand, and his long thin scissors in the other.

I leapt up and shook Figgis violently by both shoulders. All the cut hair went sliding down the smooth slope of the cloth draped round him. 'Figgis!'

But he was too far gone to respond to that name.

I shook him and yelled, shook him and yelled, and he just went on yelling back strange words, getting more and more aggressive. I took one look at Fred's horrified face and realised he was on the point of phoning for an ambulance. Everybody else had melted from the shop. They must have thought that Figgis was having an epileptic fit or something, and hadn't waited to find out. Oh, the dear, dear English!

It was time for extreme measures. I yelled, 'Latif.' Anything to bring him round; anything to avoid getting hospitals and doctors involved.

'Latif' worked. Worked insofar that he changed into English, but still went on staring round in that hot-eyed way.

'The Arabs are one people,' he said. 'The English draw lines on the map, and call us Iraqis and Kuwaitis. But the Arabs are one people. Kuwait is the nineteenth province of Iraq.'

There was only one thing to do. I ripped off the barber's cloth from round him, found three pound coins in my pocket and slammed them down on Fred's counter with the wash-hand basin, so that all his scissors jumped in the air; and hauled Figgis out of the shop.

I frog-marched him round the corner and into some bushes, holding him as tightly as a policeman making an arrest. I was yelling at him, and swearing at him, and slapping him in my panic. But he just kept on saying things like, 'The Americans will not fight. They have no stomach for close combat,' and all the other Saddam crap.

Finally, he came out of it, and there was Figgis staring sadly out of his own eyes. 'Oh, Tom, my face does hurt.' There were tears in his eyes; his eyes were awash with them. 'Tom, I feel so *tired*.'

I had to practically carry him home. And when I got him there, I found that Fred had phoned up Mum, frantic with worry.

Figgis just sat slumped in one of the lounge armchairs, while Mum and I had it out over his head.

'Look, he just fell asleep. I sometimes nearly fall asleep in Fred's. He has his shop so hot, and it's so boring. Andy just dozed off. Then he began talking in his sleep, and I couldn't get him to wake up, and Fred sort of panicked. He came out of it, walking home. He's OK now!'

But he wasn't. He was starting to fall asleep again. Suddenly I was terribly afraid. This Thing was out of control.

'I'm ringing for the doctor,' said Mum. 'He's got concussion or something. He must have bumped his head. I've seen it before. That man who was hurt in that rugby match, who suddenly began thinking that Horsie was his mother . . .'

* * *

I liked Dr Morris; we'd had him since we were little kids. He was tall and thin as a beanpole, with crinkly greying brown hair that he rumpled when he was puzzled.

He was puzzled now. 'Have you bumped your head, Andy?'

Wearily, Figgis raised his head and shook it.

'Of course, he might have bumped his head and forgotten about it. That's what can happen with concussion. Amnesia. But I certainly can't feel any bruise, and it should have left a bruise.' He gently fingered Figgis's head again, with long, pale well-washed fingers. Figgis looked so odd, with his hair all cut down one side and not the other.

'I think we'd better have him in hospital for the night. You can't be too careful with concussion. I'll get them to give him an EEG. Can I use your phone?'

Mum gestured silently towards the hall. We listened silently as he rang the hospital, and argued for a bed. He rang for an ambulance. He came back briskly and said, 'They'll be here in ten minutes. Can you pack him a bag? Just pyjamas and toothbrush and a dressing gown.'

Then he turned to me, after Mum had gone upstairs. 'You sure there's nothing you can tell me,

66

Tom?' He trusted me, man to man, making it easy to tell him.

But what could I tell him, that wouldn't sound ridiculous? Like, 'My brother becomes an Iraqi soldier in the middle of the night?' He'd have had me in hospital as well. Only a different sort of hospital . . .

'I didn't see him bang his head,' I said, a bit sullenly.

'No, I don't mean that. I mean . . . drugs or anything?'

'Andy would *never* take drugs.' That at least I could say with an honest heart. So it came out a bit too loud and glad.

He went on looking at me. It was unbearable.

'Look,' I said. 'I can't be with him every hour of the day and night.'

'No,' he said. 'You're not your brother's keeper.'

Oh, I longed to tell him, to lay the burden down. But he'd go bananas, and Mum would go bananas, and Dad would go bananas . . .

'Right,' he said. And opened his brown notebook, usually held shut with two elastic bands, and began to look up the address of his next patient. You feel so lonely when your doctor switches off, like a TV set.

Then Mum came back with Figgis's bag, and for some reason Dr Morris took her hand.

'Don't worry. It's only for a day or so. Better safe than sorry.'

How wrong can a doctor get? It was much more than a day or so. And there was no safety, only sorrow.

We all went to see Figgis that night in the hospital. He looked better, much more like his old self. He had a grin for us, and asked what books we'd brought him to read. A doctor came, and told us that they'd done the EEG, and that Figgis's brain scan was absolutely normal. Mum had brought a lot of black grapes, and I kept eating them to annoy Figgis and we squabbled comfortably about it.

It was a general sort of ward, with six beds in it. The bed next to Figgis was occupied by the oldest man I'd ever seen, so wrinkled that even his wrinkles had wrinkles. But he seemed very spry and friendly. His blue eyes twinkled at me, and he gave me a big false-toothed grin. You could see that old as he was, he still had all his marbles. He had no visitors, and Mum went across to chat to him after a while. I expect she was so glad to find Figgis better that she wanted to spread the happiness around a bit. She's like that.

While she was busy chattering away, Figgis told me the old man was a good bloke. He was ninety-two, and still rode a bicycle. But he'd fallen off it and given his head a nasty bang, and he was in for observation like Figgis. Figgis said the old boy had been in the Great War, as a soldier, and also knew a lot about fishing. Figgis didn't like fishing much, he thought it was cruel to the fish, as Mum did. But he said the old boy was good company.

So, it was a happy evening, a thank-God-it's-not-worse evening, when we sort of built a little tent of love and laughs round poor old Figgis. As we left, Dad promised him a trip to the Manchester museum, the following Saturday.

We got home, feeling all flat and relieved. Dad flopped down in his chair and began playing with the telly handset, getting his famous Teletext. Dad's hooked on Teletext like a junkie's hooked on crack. He's always flicking it on, at odd moments. It drives Mum mad. And he's always telling us little facts from it, that we don't want to know, like the British birth rate is going down. Or England have collapsed against an Australian State Eleven; again.

But that night, he suddenly said, 'Aha!' in a most vicious gleeful voice.

'What is it now?' said Mum wearily, with her eyes shut, from the couch. 'Don't tell me your British Telecom shares have gone up again?'

'It's started,' said Dad, all gloating.

'What has?'

'The air war against Iraq. That'll wipe the grin off

Saddam's face. He'll soon change his tune now.'

Mum looked wearily at the glowing message on the telly. 'It just says they're practising night air manoeuvres.'

'That's just a cover-up. It's *started*.'

Mum got up wearily. 'You want a hottie tonight, Tom?'

'Yes, please,' I said.

'Saddam's made a very bad mistake,' said Dad, not at all put out by our lack of interest. 'With the end of the Cold War, the Yanks will use every weapon they've got against him. Everything they had to stop the Ruskis. I wonder if all their gadgets will work. If they do, God help him.'

'I think you're *sick*,' called Mum viciously from the kitchen.

'It's as good a use as any for them. It'll save the Yanks having to take them home and destroy them. It'll tidy things up nicely . . .'

They had a bad row in bed that night. I heard them, as I was lying awake. Worrying about Figgis. And, oddly enough, Latif. You get into a funny state, on the edge of sleep. Dreams flick on and off, so you can't tell if you're awake or dreaming.

Eleven

Latif

We walked into the ward the following night, and Figgis wasn't there. The bed where he'd been was just a flat mattress. The bedside locker that we'd left thick with grapes and books, was empty. We thought at first we'd come to the wrong ward, they're all so much alike. But the old bloke was still there. It's a terrible feeling, seeing an empty bed in hospital. It's like a death.

'He's all right,' said the old man, looking at our faces. 'They just took him to a private room, to be on his own.'

'But why?'

'He had a funny do, in the middle of the night. I wakened up, and he was lying under his bed, all curled up in a ball, sucking his thumb and moaning. When they pulled him out, he yelled the place down. Just one word. Over and over. Sounded like "Akbar" to me. "Akbar", over and over.'

71

Mum's hand clenched white, round the handles of the shopping-bag that she was carrying, full of goodies for Figgis.

'What was wrong with him? What did they say? The doctor?'

'He didn't know what to say, except to give him a sedative. And a big injection it was, too. Rigid, he was. They carried him out, rigid, curled-up. I've only ever seen that once before in my life. In France, in the Great War. Happened to a mate of mine. We called it shell shock. He was sent home to Blighty. He was never the same again, after that. He lived for years, but he was never the same . . .'

Just then a nurse bustled up, and said the doctor wanted to see Mum and Dad. She took them off into sister's office, and the doctor came, and I watched them through the little round window in the door. I couldn't hear anything that was said. But Dad kept asking questions, and then looking down and nodding and rubbing his face like it hurt. And Mum was very pale, and still clutching that bag of goodies for Figgis, like her life depended on it.

Then we went in to see Figgis. He wasn't curled up by that time; just lying flat and staring into space, up at the ceiling. When we spoke to him, he looked at us, listlessly.

Then I could've screamed. For it wasn't even

the *ghost* of Figgis's old look. It was the hot, scared, jumpy look.

I know it sounds mad. But it wasn't Figgis lying there. It was Latif.

We were silent going home in the car. The dread word 'psychiatrist' had been mentioned by the doctor. And it hung over us like an icy cloud. With a flurry of irritation, at traffic lights, Dad switched on the radio. Not heartless, just to break the awful silence. He got some music, and a stupid amiable DJ's voice blurbing on. Radio Manchester or something. Such hilarity! Unbearable, but not as unbearable as the silence.

Then, suddenly the news at nine o'clock.

The Allied Air Forces had flown two thousand sorties. Tornadoes were attacking airfields. Two hundred cruise missiles had been launched. Iraqi front-line positions were being heavily pounded . . .

'Horsie, switch that *off* . . .' My mother's voice cracked on the edge of hysteria.

My father tried, but somehow his hands were clumsy. It seemed forever before that smug, brisk voice died away.

Twelve

Ward

It was quite different when we drove over to see Figgis at the mental hospital. We drove through pretty countryside instead of sooty buildings. The hospital lay in its own wooded grounds.

My father said he had heard it was a very liberal, enlightened place. No locked doors. The patients could wander in the grounds on fine days. People were encouraged to talk out their problems, in group discussions.

It certainly gave that impression. Ladies in nice frocks strolled in twos and threes. Some people were playing croquet on a well-mown lawn in brilliant sunlight. It could almost have been a posh hotel. Except there were two old blokes in cardigans, shut up together in a telephone kiosk, ignoring the phone and talking their heads off . . .

Plenty of parking. The doctor had said it would be easy. Mental patients didn't get daily visits, like the physically ill. There were only three cars in the car park and one, a big shiny Merc, was in the space marked 'Consultants Only'.

Our consultant was a Dr Rashid. Dad said bitterly that the NHS couldn't afford English doctors any more. Mum said tightly that she wondered if foreign doctors could be expected to understand the English mind. You could tell they were upset; but they were trying to be decent and liberal about it.

Dr Rashid had us brought into his office, as soon as we went to Reception. He was a tall, handsome man, with a smooth creamy face and hair so black it shone blue. I hate to think how much his suit cost, but I forgave him, because his face was kind. His English was very good, rather public-school, except that he had to twist his mouth oddly to make one or two of our sounds.

'You must understand, Mr and Mrs Higgins, that you will find your son much changed. And you must understand we have undertaken no treatment yet – just sedatives, and observation. We do not rush in where angels fear to tread! Let me also stress that the way you will find him is the way he wishes to be at present. The way in which he is most comfortable. He is calm at the moment – you will be able to go and see him presently. But first a few questions . . . Please, where did your son learn to speak Arabic?'

There was an utter silence. He might as well have asked when poor Figgis first turned into an elephant.

Then my father said angrily, 'Arabic? He can't speak any Arabic. There must be some mistake – you've got the wrong kid.' He got to his feet, as if he was going to leap out and rescue Figgis from this place where everyone, even the psychiatrist, must be mad. My mother put out a pale hand to restrain him.

Dr Rashid put up his own creamy, slim hands in a gesture that was half soothing, and half almost a prayer. 'Calm yourself, Mr Higgins. I do assure you your son is speaking Arabic. I do not speak it myself, but I have worked in the Gulf States and I recognise it, as you might recognise French or German.'

I thought my dad was going to hit him. As if speaking Arabic was even worse than being mad. So I blurted out, 'Andy has been talking a funny language, Dad. In his sleep.'

My father turned his terrifying glare on me instead.

'Why didn't you tell us this?'

'I didn't think you'd believe me,' I quavered.

'Let us sit down and discuss this calmly,' said Dr Rashid. 'Who is Akbar? Is he perhaps an Arab boy whom he has met at your Elmborough Grammar School? I know they have boys of several races there.'

He was right, too. We've got three Japanese, two Koreans and a lot of Pakistanis. But I'd never heard of an Arab, and I was sure I would have done, if there'd been one. Still, this Dr Rashid was no fool. I began to have hope, looking at his keen intelligent face, and his posh stainless steel Biro, poised over a sheet of clean paper.

'Go on,' said my father abruptly, as if he was feeling a bit the same way about him.

'We get very little – very few English words – out of your son. But he speaks quite a lot of Arabic. To himself, when he is alone. Almost as if he thought there were others round him . . .'

'Go on,' said my father again, as the silence grew deeper.

'I have an Arab friend in London – another psychiatrist. I thought we might send for him, with your permission. If he were to talk to your son in Arabic, we might learn more of your son's illness . . .

'It could not be on the National Health Service, of course. He would have to make a long journey, and we need him quickly. It would not be cheap. And, alas, it might all come to nothing. But I think it is worth trying . . .'

'How much?' asked my father. I could tell he was suspicious of all foreigners; suspicious of being taken for a ride.

'Alas, five hundred pounds. My friend is a top specialist. He would give the whole day . . .'

'I'll pay,' said my father. What else could he say?

After a lot more questions, that I won't bore you with, because in the end they had nothing to do with it, Dr Rashid took us to see Figgis.

He was in a room by himself. With a locked door.

He was sitting cross-legged on the floor, in the corner, beneath the window. He was wearing tee-shirt, denims, socks and trainers; his own. He had pulled his bed very close to him, in the corner. And turned the mattress so it spanned the gap between the bed and the windowsill. He sat in a sort of little shelter he'd made for himself. In one hand, he clutched a short broom with a broken handle, such as you might find in any hospital cleaner's cupboard. He clutched it, leaned into it as he had leaned into the air gun in our bedroom that night. Another odd thing was that he had tucked his jeans inside his socks. The oddest thing of all was that he was wearing a hat, pulled down hard over his ears. Some sort of sun hat, once bright orange in colour, now faded and old and stained.

He did not notice us; or if he did, he didn't let on. Certainly he never looked at us. Instead his hot-looking eyes roamed ceaselessly. Most of the time close to the floor; and it was then he muttered inaudible words. But every so often, he would let his eyes wander round the ceiling. As if watching for something, or listening for something. As if watching and listening to some invisible sky far above the plaster ceiling.

At his feet lay a bowl, the sort of stainless steel bowl that hospitals use; it was empty, but had little bits of stuff caked hard round the rim. I had a feeling there'd been food in it.

'Do not upset yourself,' said Dr Rashid. 'We have not done this to him. He has done this all for himself. He got the broom from a cupboard in the corridor, before we locked the door. I don't know where he got the hat from. If we leave him this way, he is peaceful most of the time. If we try to move him . . .' He paused, with an elegant shrug that hid many horrors, many efforts, much pain. Then he added, 'There he feels safe, I think.'

Of course, my parents went across to Figgis, called his name; Mum took him by the hand; Dad shook him by the shoulder. He just swayed, like a statue that is being shaken. And his eyes never looked at them, just continued their restless, suspicious journey around the room.

'C'mon, Andy,' said my father. 'For God's sake, snap out of it. You've got me and your mum worried sick. Stop playing these silly games . . .'

No effect. My father shook him harder; picked him

up bodily by the shoulders and stood glaring into his face. 'Andy, for God's sake, Andy!'

Still his eyes wandered around the room. They were not in the same world. My father shook him harder still, shouting so they could have heard him all over the hospital.

Dr Rashid laid a gentle, manicured hand on my father's arm. 'Please, Mr Higgins, it is *useless*.'

For a long time, the three of them stood together, as if all were frozen. Then my father made a sound of disgust, deep in his throat, and pushed Figgis away from him.

Quite unperturbed, Figgis resumed his sitting position, and began his restless watch of the non-existent sky again.

'What the hell . . .?' roared my father.

'Please, Mr Higgins, not here. We will disturb other patients. Let us go back to my office.'

Back in the office, my father paced up and down like a caged tiger. He kept flexing his great powerful hands. He wanted to hit something, to smash something. But it was only that, perhaps for the first time in his life, he felt totally helpless. All his world was *physical*. He was a builder, a repairer, and there was nothing to build or mend. He was a fighter, and there was no one to fight. He was as brave as a lion; feared no man living; but it was as if something had come out of the dark, that he couldn't see, or even touch. It was so cruel I could have wept for him. Finally, all his courage ran out with his energy, and he just collapsed into a chair and stared at the wall in silence.

All this time my mother had been sitting silent, just playing with the handles of the plastic carrier, twisting them tight as ropes. Now Dr Rashid turned his attention to her.

'Is it . . . schizophrenia?' she asked. She had to force out the word, syllable by syllable.

'Mrs Higgins, I do not know,' said Dr Rashid, gently. 'It does not correspond to any case of schizophrenia I have ever seen. He is not the usual age for the onset of schizophrenia – usually it comes on later than this . . . seventeen or eighteen . . . twenty. They are usually sixth formers or students . . .'

Mum bit her lip, hard. Figgis was always her special one, because after she had him, the doctor told her she couldn't have any more. She understood Figgis better than Dad; Figgis was more like her, whereas I take after Dad. Always before, she had been able to make things right for Figgis. But now, for all her work with social problems, all her healing skills with animals, she was just as helpless as Dad. It was the first time I'd ever seen both my parents helpless; it's a bit terrifying, the first time.

Dr Rashid said gently, 'You will have to trust me, Mrs Higgins. We will look after him, as well as we can. The human mind has great powers of self-healing. We shall not rush in hastily with . . . *treatment*; we shall keep him safe and as calm as possible, and observe. I will let you know before we begin any . . . *treatment*. We shall have to have your consent anyway.'

They looked into each other's eyes a long time. Then my mother said, 'I trust you, Dr Rashid,' and got to her feet and shook hands with him. Gathering up her gloves she said, 'C'mon, Horsie. Let's leave the doctor to get on with his work. He knows best.'

My father got to his feet like a lamb. He shook hands with Dr Rashid, but he didn't look him in the eye. He kept his eyes on the floor, as if he was ashamed, humiliated, a beaten man. I had never seen my father look beaten before. He suddenly looked so *old*. They both looked so old . . .

And I felt it was all my fault. Why had I played those games with Figgis's mind, while he was asleep? Why had I mucked about with the Latif thing? Why had I asked him all those questions? It had been a kind of sick hunger. A hunger for kicks. I'd played with his mind as if it was some cheap plastic toy. Not caring about him. Not caring he was my brother, who I'd always looked after. And now, maybe, I'd destroyed him. I wanted to confess, like some criminal. I felt I *was* a criminal. And a much worse criminal than some unemployed bloke who breaks in to steal tellies and videos. That seemed a clean thing to do, by comparison with what I'd done.

Dr Rashid's receptionist rang through to say the next set of parents were waiting . . . It was now or never. I must do something to rescue Figgis. But what?

What I did was to leave my scarf on the floor by my chair. Halfway back to the car, I told Mum and Dad I was going back for it.

Dr Rashid was sitting with his head in his hands. I think he was charging up his batteries for the next consultation. But he looked up at me, without surprise. 'I have been rather expecting you! Your scarf is where you left it.' He had a nice smile, just a bit weary. It was a smile you could tell anything to.

I said, 'He thinks he's an Iraqi soldier out in the Gulf. He'll answer to the name of "Latif". You can call him out with it, and he'll talk to you in English. You can also try calling him "Figgis" – that's his pet name, that's what I call him. Do you think I'm mad, for telling you this?'

He gave me his sad sweet, weary tolerant smile again. 'I think half the world is mad, Tom. But I do not include you in that number. How long has it been going on?'

'Since last August,' I said. Then, 'All his life! I've got so much to tell you . . .'

'Not now,' he said warningly. 'Your parents will be wondering where you've got to. And they've had enough for one day. I will get in touch with you . . . now be off. I have other patients also.'

But he finally made some notes on his blank sheet of paper, with his posh Biro.

I went back to the car feeling a bit better. Confession is good for the soul, they say, don't they?

That was the last time I was to feel better; 'til the end.

Thirteen

Rashid

I almost didn't notice Dr Rashid's Merc outside our school gates, the following Monday evening. I sort of jerked and bumped through the school days, in fits and starts, between thinking about Figgis. But once I passed out through the school gates I would just brood about Figgis with my head down, all the way home. It's a wonder I wasn't knocked down and killed, stepping out in front of a bus.

But I saw Dr Rashid sitting in his car, waiting for me, and my heart turned right over. I knew it was something big that had brought him here. But good or bad? As I stood there, he beckoned to me, and I went across and opened the big solid door of the Merc, bracing myself, not able to say anything because I suddenly had no breath.

It was at that point that Jason Bratt and his nasty little mob swept up. Bratt must have taken in the shiny car, Dr Rashid's posh suit and Dr

Rashid's face in one swift glance.

'Getting off with a Wog poofter, Higgins?'

His little gang gave the expected snigger. I whirled round and made the amazing discovery that I wanted to knock Bratt down and hammer his head against the edge of the pavement until it cracked open like a bloody egg. All the misery about Figgis came flooding up in a sea of hate.

'I'll kill you, Bratt!' I was so mad it came out in a cloud of spit that settled on his lapels. He brushed his lapels down ostentatiously, for the benefit of his gang. But he saw the look I gave him, and that wiped the grin off him.

'Suit yourself,' he sort of choked out, to save his face. But I've never seen him vanish so quickly.

'Get in,' said Dr Rashid. He had to reach over and close my door for me, I was shaking so much. Then we drove off, and I never even noticed where we were going, until I found we were parked in a lay-by on the bypass.

'You don't mind being seen here with a Wog poofter?' asked Dr Rashid. He was trying to make a joke of it for my sake, but his voice had a bit of a tremble in it too. I expect it was rage.

'I'll kill him,' I said. 'I'll *kill* him!'

'No, you won't. Don't be silly,' said Dr Rashid. We sat for a moment in silence.

Then he said, rather sadly, 'I am a member of the Royal College of Psychiatrists. I give them lectures. I have a big car and make much money. But I am still a Wog poofter. There is no exam I can pass that exempts me from being a Wog poofter.'

'I apologise for my country . . .'

'All countries are the same.' He threw it off with a shrug, an effort, then said, 'I did not come to discuss racists. I came to tell you about your brother. Can you spare half an hour, or will it make your parents worried? I will run you to the end of your road, afterwards . . .'

'That's OK. They won't worry for half an hour.'

He swallowed three times, then said, 'My friend has been up. He had a long talk with your brother.' Then he didn't seem able to go on.

'Well?' I said.

'He had a long talk with the personality you called "Latif". But as "Latif" he totally convinced my friend. He speaks good Arabic, the Arabic of central Iraq, the district called Babylon, around Baghdad . . . Latif Al-Bakr Takriti is his full name. He is thirteen years old, and a soldier in an armoured brigade of the Iraqi army. He gave his army number – it is a quite possible number. My friend was a doctor in the Iraqi Army long ago, before Saddam Hussein. He spoke to "Latif" in the manner of an officer. "Latif" answered all his questions in the manner of a soldier; standing to attention. He spoke of his friends, who live in the same foxhole in Kuwait, near the Saudi border. His friends are the shepherd Akbar, Ali Hadda who comes from Basra . . . there is even one called "Saddam". "Saddam" is a common name in Iraq.'

'But . . . how is it possible?'

'I wish I knew. If I wrote these things in my case notes, I would be struck off as a lunatic myself. Yet it is so. I cannot deny it. Oh . . .' he flung out an arm in a despairing gesture, 'there are cases recorded in plenty, of telepathy. There has been much research. People who have known the moment when a loved one has died, even though they were a thousand miles away at the time . . . people who have even felt the loved one's pain. There are links between minds that medical science will not acknowledge; that are beyond science. But I have not time to tell you of them now.

'My problem is . . . your father is paying five hundred pounds to my friend. What am I going to tell *him*?'

'He'd go bonkers if you told him that,' I said. 'He'd take Figgis . . . Andy . . . away from you. To another hospital.'

'That is what I feared. And other doctors, with closed minds, would say Andy had this or that mental disease, and fill him up with drugs, or put electrodes on his head, to cure him. When he is not sick.

'Your brother is not mad, Tom. He suffers from a mystery of nature . . . But what am I to do about it?'

'Keep quiet. Say your friend is delayed . . . ill . . . can't come yet. Play for time.'

'You think time will cure it?'

'Well, it started with this war. It might stop if the war ends, and Latif goes home. Once the crisis is over.' I explained about Figgis and Bossa. 'Figgis does get over things quickly, once the crisis is over.'

'But Figgis did not think he *was* Bossa! What if "Latif" gets killed . . .?'

'What? A young kid of that age?'

'From what I hear there are a lot of kids under fifteen in the Iraqi army. Kids under fifteen who are waiting to kill Americans, many Americans. Latif has got over his first fear; of the bombing. He is resigned now, to dying. But he hopes he can kill an American first. If he can kill two or three, he will die happy.'

It made me feel sick, when he said that. 'Why *do* they hate the Americans so much? What have the Americans ever done to them?'

'Latif says the Americans want to eat up the whole world. All the oil, rubber, tin. So they can sit with four cars in each garage. And no one can stop them, except Saddam Hussein. The Germans tried to fight the

89

Americans, and now they are American puppets. So are the Japanese. The Vietnamese beat the Americans once, but now the Americans blockade them and starve their children to death. He talks of San Salvador and Nicaragua . . . to "Latif" the Americans are ravening monsters, who know no God but greed . . . he wishes to die bravely, fighting the monsters.'

'What does he think of the British?' Somehow I had to ask.

'He says the British are the Americans' little dog, which barks when its master tells it to.'

'They're mad,' I said. 'They haven't got a prayer . . .'

'What about you British in 1940? You hadn't got a prayer. Were you mad, to defy Hitler?'

I couldn't think of anything to say.

Dr Rashid said gently, 'I know how they feel. They are tired of the world calling them Wog poofters. Suddenly, it is better to be dead, than to go on being a Wog poofter. Once the Arabs had a great empire, that stretched from India to the Atlantic. They were the first scientists. "Algebra" is an Arabic word. Your maths are done with Arabic numerals. They invented the compass, and astronomy and the beginnings of medicine. In the Arabic University of Granada in Spain, Muslims and Christians and Jews worked together in peace, to establish the truths of science. Until the Inquisition came . . . You wanted to kill this

90

Jason Bratt, because he called me a Wog poofter. Suppose you and your father and your grandfather had been called that? For generations. Would you kill then?'

'But Saddam Hussein's a murderer . . .'

'He is an Arab who has shaken the world. They would forgive him anything for that.'

'Oh, God, I feel sick.'

'I'm sorry. I will drive you home. You are too young to bear such burdens . . .'

He started the engine, and put the car into gear. It was starting to rain, and he switched on the Merc's big single windscreen-wiper. I watched it swinging, like the pendulum of time itself; and us, the raindrops, wiped away.

At the end of our road, he reached over again and opened the door for me. 'I will try to keep your brother safe and calm. He is not unhappy at present. He just sits in his shelter, watching the sky. He eats quite well. We feed him rice in a bowl . . .'

'But if "Latif" is in Figgis's body, where is Figgis?' It just burst out of me.

Dr Rashid looked at me straight. 'If "Latif" is in Figgis's body, maybe Figgis is in Latif's body, in the foxhole. Maybe they live in both bodies, together . . . it is a dreadful thought for you. But you would soon have thought it for yourself. I don't know. It is a mystery.'

I walked into the house only ten minutes late. Mum was upstairs hoovering the bedrooms. I yelled, over the noise of the Hoover, 'I'm home!'

'I'll be down in a minute. I'll make you a cup of tea.'

I could tell from the gladness in her voice that she'd been worrying about me. When one chick's in danger, you worry twice as much about the other.

The big telly in the lounge was on. I think it was only on to break up the silence in the house for Mum. Some silly children's programme was just finishing. Then there came a newsflash about Kuwait, and I just had to watch it.

Old Norman, Stormin' Norman, in news conference, looking as big as a cliff, and as certain as God in gold-rimmed spectacles.

'What are we going to do about Saddam's army? I'll tell you what we're going to do about Saddam's army. First we're going to cut it off, and then we're going to kill it. But not 'til we're ready . . .'

Not 'til they've been bombed to bits, I thought. Oh, Figgis. Latif . . .

Fourteen

Faces

I saw things differently after that. The faces on the telly, I mean, for I watched the telly non-stop.

Saddam Hussein, the big-paunched swagger, the knowing, cocky grin under the big black moustache. I knew he was a bully, a braggart, a killer, a mass murderer, an utterly evil man. And yet he didn't really look like that. He looked . . . human. Like a used-car dealer you wouldn't trust an inch, and yet you might have a drink with him in a pub, and listen to his stories. You felt you'd be OK, if you didn't cross him. Or do business with him. As I said, human.

The allied military spokesmen, they were the ones who terrified me. With their cropped hair and still, expressionless faces and drab combat gear, they looked like monks. They never swaggered, or bullied or boasted. It was far beneath them. They talked coolly and humbly in their strange religious jargon. 'Friendly fire.' 'Ground and aerial assets.' 'Tactical penetration.' They might have been talking about Holy Unction or transcendental meditation.

The humble monks of death.

Saddam had slain his thousands.

They were going to slay their ten thousands.

Not for pride or rage or hate.

For oil.

As the days passed, I watched my parents turn into old, old people. My dad's paunch, which had seemed sort of prosperous and cheeky, turned to just saggy. The lines in his face got deeper. I thought he was going balder, faster. I was afraid he'd soon be as bald as an egg.

My mother just gave up her council work, resigned. I don't think she could face meeting people, and having them ask about Figgis, and whisper about Figgis behind her back. To everyone else, Figgis was in a mental hospital and therefore Figgis was mad.

After a few days, Dr Rashid had a gentle talk with them. Told them they should stop coming to see Figgis; it was just making him worse. But he said I should go on coming; Figgis and I had this special bond, and I might get through to him . . .

I thought this was pretty hard on my parents, especially my mum, and the first time I biked over to see Figgis on my own, I said so to Dr Rashid.

He smiled and nodded, as if he didn't disagree. Then he said, 'I have to think about your brother – what will make him happier. Come and see what he is doing.'

As soon as I got into Figgis's big empty room, I saw what he meant. It wasn't empty any more. They had supplied Figgis with a lot of hospital junk – old mattresses, broken chairs, a huge number of old stained saggy pillows. And with them, very neatly, Figgis had built defences. Mattresses were laid three feet deep over the place where he sat. There was a wall of pillows, piled up like sandbags. There was the line of a trench, and a firing position.

'This is how it must be, out in the Kuwaiti desert,' said Dr Rashid. 'And see what I have got for him . . .'

Figgis sat in a pair of camouflage trousers, gaiters and boots. The boots were highly polished. On his top, over a sweat shirt, he wore an open combat jacket. On his head, an old American steel helmet from World War II, with the straps hanging loose. And he leaned against some old sort of gun, a rifle, but I don't know what kind of rifle it was.

'He spends much time, cleaning his boots and his gun,' said Dr Rashid. 'All this work is much better for him than just sitting. He is happier, he will wash now. And he eats more. In his own way, he is content.'

'How did you manage all this?'

Dr Rashid gave his sad smile. 'I am quite famous. People humour me, because I write learned books. It did not cost them anything. And army and navy stores are wonderful places. And I have a friend who collects militaria.'

'But won't this make him more . . .?' I couldn't bring myself to say the word.

'Mad?' He said the word for me. 'But we have agreed, you and I, that he is not mad. That he is suffering from a mystery of nature. Why should he not suffer in more comfort? Will you stay with him a while, and remember anything he says? Ring for a nurse, if you wish to be let out.'

So he left, locking the door behind him. And I sat next to Figgis. I wasn't afraid of him; he was my brother. But it was weird. For he was never still. He looked up, he greeted people, with a tense little lopsided grin, in what I now knew was Arabic. He waved to invisible passers-by; once he even laughed at what some invisible person must have said.

And all the time he watched the sky, with his ears cocked, and I thought of Stormin' Norman.

After a while, it was almost as if I was sitting in a trench with him, out in Kuwait. My eyes followed his eyes; I grinned when he grinned. I watched invisible figures pass with him, until they almost became real to me too. And I began to be tense and tight-stomached. Not because I was in a mental hospital with a sick brother, but because I, too, was waiting to fight and kill Americans.

It was pretty tiring, this switching back and forth between here and there. Reminding myself that the sudden sound of jet engines in the real sky above the hospital was just a passing jumbo jet. I think I must have dozed; for I came to with a start when I heard a voice whisper, 'Tom?'

'Figgis!'

He was looking at me slyly, sideways. He raised a finger to his lips, as if he was afraid we might be overheard.

I was mad with joy, but I kept my voice down, afraid he might vanish again. Because it really was Figgis, with his straight way of looking at you.

'Figgis! Have you come back? For good?'

He shook his head. 'Only got a minute.'

'Are you OK?'

'Yeah, I'm OK. They're nice guys. They look after Latif – treat him like a mascot. There's six of them, and they stick together. Akbar's a good bloke, like Dad. Strong. He's the corporal in charge. He's older than the rest of us. He's got one grandchild, only a baby. I've seen her photo. Then there's Rez – he's a clown. Gives impersonations of the major, behind his back, when he's not looking. Makes us laugh. Then there's

Ali – he's got a wife and two little girls. Spends hours writing to them, only there's no way to post the letters . . .'

'What the hell are *you* doing there? Do they know about you?'

'No. I'm sort of part of Latif; inside Latif, watching. Latif's stronger than me. I just watch what's going on . . .'

'Can't you get back? Back to us here?'

'Latif's too strong. I can only come now because he's dozing. We don't get any real sleep – they bomb us every night to keep us awake. Everybody keeps dozing off all the time. Two blokes were found asleep on sentry duty. They shot them, and they made us watch. It was horrible.'

'Figgis – what are we going to do?'

'Nothing we can do. I'm trapped, Tom. I don't understand it. All our world just faded away, and I was here. I've tried to get back, but I can't.'

'But it's *impossible* . . .'

'It's happened, Tom. I only hope it doesn't happen to anybody else.'

'But it's so *unfair*! What have you done to deserve this?'

'What's fair, Tom? The world's not fair. Do you think Akbar and Ali want to be here, any more than I do? All they want is to get back to their families . . .'

'Why don't they . . . surrender?'

'Minefields in front, and death squads behind. Some of the guys tried it. They brought them back and shot them too. And we had to watch. God, Tom, this is a terrible place . . .'

I looked at his face. He was quite utterly desperate, in a very quiet way. Then he said, 'I sometimes think . . .' and then paused.

'*What*?'

'That I'm meant to be here, to see it all. To make up for all those who're watching on the TV as if it was a soap . . .'

I remembered the newsreel that Stormin' Norman had shown the press, about 'The luckiest man in Iraq' – the film footage of an air attack on a bridge, and the bridge blowing up, and the car on the bridge that had just escaped in time. And how all the TV reporters had laughed.

'Is there anything I can *do*?' I asked, without hope.

'You can listen . . . and remember afterwards. Tell people what it was like. I *want* people to know what it was like. Latif and Akbar and Ali are people too . . .'

'But *you* can tell them – when it's all over. When you come home . . .'

He was silent; and suddenly I was very scared; more scared than I'd ever been in my life.

'Figgis – you still there?'

'Yes, Tom. Just. But . . . people won't believe me when I come home; they'll just say I was potty . . .'

For some reason, from the sad look on his face, and I've never seen any kid look sadder, I knew he was lying to comfort me.

'Figgis . . . you are *coming* back?'

'Tom . . . I don't know how. I'm getting weaker and weaker, and Latif's getting stronger and stronger. I don't think I'll ever get back. I think we're all going to die, Tom.'

'NO. I WON'T LET YOU.' I grabbed him by both wrists.

But he threw off my hands with the viciousness of a stranger. And when I looked at his face, it was the face of Latif again. Latif had woken up. Once he had got rid of my hands he gazed around warily at the sky, then yawned and stretched like a cat. Then he began to clean the gun with a piece of rag that lay nearby.

The gun was already very shiny; I got the feeling he was just polishing it to keep busy, to stop himself thinking.

Fifteen

Death

That was the Friday night. I sat on a bit longer, in hopes that Figgis would come back. I didn't have school next day, anyway. After a while, I seemed to sense a change in the body of my brother. He edged deeper and deeper into the shelter he'd made for himself. Crouched up more, as if he was trying to make himself as small as possible. Kept putting his hands over his ears. I knew that things were getting rougher for him. Very rough indeed. By the end he was lying on his side like a scrunched-up ball, hands over his ears all the time, and eyes tight shut.

I knew they were being bombed, bad. I could see the explosions of the bombs in the flinching of his body. How often had he lain like that, unseen, over the nights, while I lay safe and snug at home in bed? A whole war inside one small body. I knelt forward and put both hands on him, and he suddenly sort of wriggled into my arms, as if I were his living shelter.

Was it Figgis or Latif? I didn't know, for he was beyond speaking. In the end, I didn't care. I curled up round him in his little shelter, and felt him shake. I hated the Americans.

I don't know how long I would have lain there, if the light hadn't suddenly got brighter. I looked round, and there was Dr Rashid by the door, switching on all the overhead lights. He saw the two of us curled up together, and he looked suddenly terrified.

'Tom? Tom? You OK?'

'Just about,' I managed to say. I tried to free myself a bit from Figgis's body, but he was clutching me so tight I couldn't. So Dr Rashid had to kneel on the floor beside me.

'I heard the nine o'clock news,' said Dr Rashid. 'It's as well I did. I'd forgotten you were here, locked in. You should have rung for one of the nurses, she'd have let you out.'

'I don't want to leave him,' I said. 'He's bad.'

'I've never seen him as bad as this. I think it's started, the land war. They report carpet-bombing all along the front line . . .'

'I'm staying,' I said. 'Can you ring up my mum and dad? Say you're expecting a medical breakthrough or something, and I'm staying the night.'

He looked very doubtful. 'Are you sure this is wise?'

'Try and stop me,' I gritted. 'Anyway, I couldn't get loose without breaking his fingers.'

'I will go and ring your parents, and then come back and be with you too. I will bring something to eat and drink.'

I heard his footsteps walking away, and the key turn in the lock. And then I was back in the hell with Figgis again.

I came awake, in the grey light of dawn. My arms were empty. But the stink in the room . . . and my clothes were wet.

'Your brother has wet himself . . . and . . .'

'Shit himself, too,' I said. 'Where is he?' I should have felt disgust. But somehow it didn't matter. It was too late to matter.

'Standing by the window. He has not moved for an hour.'

I went across and touched his arm. He was as stiff as a statue again.

'Figgis,' I called. 'Figgis. Figgis, old mate.'

The fourth time I spoke and touched him, he gave a little start, as if coming awake.

'Tom?' His voice was weaker and further away than ever.

'I'm here, old mate.' I grabbed him by both arms.

'Rez and Ali went to fetch food. They didn't come

back. I went to look for them. Everyone is dead back there. They are all in pieces; arms, legs, heads still inside steel helmets. Hands. How can they bury them, if they are all in pieces . . . hundreds of them? Thousands . . . How are they going to *bury* them?'

Then he began crying, in the most terrible and hopeless way. My own body began to shake, and I couldn't stop it.

'Enough,' said Dr Rashid. 'Or I will not be responsible. You must eat, Tom, and we must get you cleaned up. Come to my quarters. I will order breakfast. The staff nurse will give your brother a sedative, so he can be cleaned up as well. I insist.'

He unlocked the door, and yelled along the corridor for a staff nurse.

I let myself be led away. Somehow I didn't think it was the right thing to do. But I no longer had the strength to argue.

To my amazement, by the time I'd had a bath and changed into some of Dr Rashid's casuals, I did feel hungry. I suppose the animal in you gets to be the boss in the end.

Of course, we watched the never-ending newscasts while we ate. The land war had started. Endless shots of pink tanks flowing through orange sand berms and streaming out across the empty puce desert with their pennants fluttering. Any other time, I'd have felt like cheering. It looked like the end of that film *Stagecoach*, where the Red Indians have surrounded the stagecoach, and the whites have run out of ammunition, and even John Wayne doesn't know what to do. And then there's a distant note of a bugle among the war-whoops of the Redskins, and there's the U.S. Seventh Cavalry streaming to the rescue, with all the pennants flying and the bugler puffing out his cheeks on horseback, fit to bust . . .

And then we had an item about some Americans burying a dead Iraqi soldier.

'That is the first dead Iraqi I have seen,' said Dr Rashid. 'In all these weeks of newsreel, one dead Iraqi.'

'Stormin' Norman doesn't believe in body counts . . . He said so.'

'This is the first war in which we have been afraid to tell how *many* we have killed. Do you think the public believe what they are seeing? Are they all little children, to believe fairy tales? Or do they not *want* to know?'

The news changed items abruptly. Something about the newspapers getting angry because certain members of the Royal Family were enjoying themselves too much in wartime.

'Ah, but there is true feeling,' said Dr Rashid. 'True patriotic feeling. The Royals must not enjoy themselves. It doesn't matter about everybody else.'

'I think I want to get back to Figgis,' I said.

'They will ring me from the ward, if there is any change . . .'

'I want to be beside Figgis. It's the only place I feel clean.'

Figgis said one last thing before the end. He said (and his voice was so faint I could hardly hear it): 'Latif's all right. He's still got Akbar. Akbar is trying to find something to make a white flag with. It's night, now. They will try to surrender the moment it gets light. But it's very hard to find something white in the dark . . . There's nobody else around here. They're all either dead or gone. We are looking for something white, but we can hear the helicopters somewhere out there. We cannot see them, but they can see us in the dark. They are like cowardly ghosts, hiding in the dark. That's what Latif thinks. Cowardly ghosts who kill. He still wants to shoot one gunship down, before he dies. Akbar tries to give him hope, but Latif knows he is going to die . . .'

My brother stopped, and the look of Latif came back across his features, and I knew it was no use.

After that, Dr Rashid and I just sat, and watched my brother's body prowl. It reminded me of some poor little creature in a cage at a wildlife park I once saw. The little thing ran up and down the front wire of its cage, back and forwards, never stopping. It took me a while to realise there was no purpose in its running. It never stopped to rest or eat. It just ran without point because its mind was totally gone. Latif was very like that, except he still carried his rifle, was still looking for an American to kill.

The prowling went on so long, it became sort of mesmerising. So that the end took us by surprise.

Suddenly my brother screamed, 'Akbar, Akbar.' And then he knelt beside something invisible on the ground, and pawed at it, as if he was . . . trying to roll it over. But every time he touched it, his hands drew back as if they'd been burnt by the thing he was touching. And the thing he was trying to touch kept on rolling away from him, and he kept on crawling after it, and burning his hands again . . .

Afterwards, I knew it must have been the body of Akbar, writhing in flames.

And then, after forever, it was over.

My brother's body stepped back. Looked around, saw the fake gun lying on the ground.

He tried to pick it up. But he couldn't. He tried over and over again.

In the end I realised he couldn't pick it up because, somewhere out there, Latif had burnt his own hands away, trying to reach burning Akbar.

Then my brother rose to his full height, and raised his burned hands, and screamed abuse at the black night sky of Kuwait. At the Americans, who lurked in darkness, and would not come to be killed, even when Latif had nothing left to kill them with.

And then his own body was writhing, being tossed into the far corner of the room, not, it seemed, by its own power, but by the power of something that was tearing it to bits. And there it lay, a little untidy bundle.

I could not go over. I knew my brother was dead.

It took Dr Rashid to go across.

And I heard, quite clearly, Figgis say, 'Where am I?' And his voice was surprisingly strong. Just baffled. Not at all like the way he'd said things before.

I went across, though all the world whirled round my head. Figgis looked across at me and said, quite cheerfully, 'Hello, Tom, I must have been asleep. What's this place?'

'It's a hospital,' I said, because I couldn't think what else to say.

'Have I been in an accident?' asked Figgis. 'I ache all over! Was I riding my bike?'

It was then I realised that he was clean and free; remembered nothing.

'He can't remember,' I muttered warningly to Dr Rashid.

'Allah be praised,' said Dr Rashid. 'If it is true. Only time will tell.'

'Is that coffee, in that Thermos flask?' asked Figgis. 'And can I have those sandwiches?' He dug into the curling-edged sandwiches as if there was no tomorrow. And I just sat and watched him.

'I shall tell your parents nothing,' said Dr Rashid. 'Agreed?'

'Agreed,' I said.

'He has been ill, and now he is better. We keep him another week, but just for observation?'

'Right.'

'He can play croquet, and amuse my old ladies . . .'

'Right.'

'He is a nice boy. I'm sure he won't mind. I shall tell him, and your parents, that he had a brainstorm, brought on by overwork. He is to take it easier in future.'

'Right,' I said, pretty doubtfully.

'What else can I say?' He shrugged, elegantly. 'What else would they believe?'

'Do you think he was mad? At all?'

'No, I do not think he was mad at all. I think he was too sane. He felt too much for his fellow men. It is the rest of the world that is mad. But do not dare to quote me on that.'

'I suppose . . . out there . . . they are all dead?'

'You mean Latif and Akbar, Ali and Rez and Saddam? I should think so. We have no way of ever finding out. Even the great Stormin' Norman has not the means to find out. Among so many dead . . . only Allah knows. The sand will bury them; or the bulldozers. Unless the stray dogs eat them for breakfast. And the wife of Ali and the daughter of Akbar will wait . . .'

'I just feel sick . . .'

'You cannot be sick now. Here are your parents, getting out of their car. Do not spoil their day of gladness. They have done no wrong . . .'

My mother and father knocked on his door, and then came in. They looked a lot better than when I'd last seen them. They looked weary, but they'd live.

'A day of good news,' said my father, shaking Dr Rashid by the hand and looking him in the eye. 'My lad on the mend, and Saddam Hussein on the run . . .'

It was truly amazing how straight Dr Rashid kept his face.

Sixteen

Return

Well, that was months ago. Nothing's really happened since. Except our family's changed. Dad hasn't played rugger since, and he doesn't go out drinking much with clients any more. His business seems to have gone quiet too, though maybe that's just the recession. Dad just seems glad to get home by five, be with us, and watch Andy out of the corner of his eye. Most of the time he seems happy, if Andy's happy. Sometimes I see a little worried frown, though he tries to hide it.

Mum hasn't gone back to helping people either. It seems to have knocked all the stuffing out of her; though she still looks after our family jolly well. In the evenings she just likes to sit on the settee with Dad and watch Andy without him noticing. She and Dad hold hands a lot more than they used to. Our house feels like a right little, tight little island, with everyone glad to be together and alive.

But the big change is in Figgis. Or should I say Andy, because we don't see Figgis any more? No more funny little ways; no more talk of dreams or daydreams, no more interesting revelations or hurt frogs brought home for Mum to look after. No more crises. You just couldn't have a more normal kid; he's normal with knobs on. Wanted a mountain bike, which of course he got straight away. Wanted a portable CD to play his glam-rock discs on. Got that too. Fond of his grub. Back to the top of the class in school work. Even starting to look at girls. He'll be wanting to play rugby next . . . Because he's getting quite big and beefy. I used to think he took after Mum, but he's getting more like Dad every day. Even getting popular at school; and no one dares to tease him.

I can almost see another Horsie Higgins in the making. More of a chip off the old block than I am.

He never remembered a thing, of all that had happened to him. As far as he is concerned, he had a brainstorm from overwork, fell off his bike and had a spell in hospital. That's what Mum and Dad let him go on believing. And God help any kid who dares to mention it to him now.

But I think it's more than forgetting; amnesia. In my heart of hearts, I think the part that was Figgis died out there, with Latif and Akbar. And nobody remembers now but me; and maybe good old Dr

112

Rashid. They're all so busy forgetting; like the world is so busy forgetting, now that Stormin' Norman is back home, playing at being a happy grandfather and dog-owner . . .

I miss Figgis more than I can say. I'm lonely without him. Most lonely when I'm with Andy. Lonely and bored with Andy. He's too much like Dad these days, too much like me. It's like living with a clone of myself. We've at last moved into separate bedrooms. Why not? There are plenty of spare bedrooms in this house. There's no reason for us to stay together. Andy doesn't need me any more.

And suddenly I'm scared; because nobody seems to give a damn about anything outside our house any more. Not hurt squirrels or starving people in Africa, or the families in trouble, who used to come to see Mum. Who's looking after them all now?

Figgis was our conscience. For all his maddening ways, we *needed* him.

All around us there are gulfs; between people. Figgis was the one who tried to build bridges over them.

Am I the only one who still cares? I hear the kids at school. Half have forgotten about the Gulf War already; the rest are just hoping that Saddam will do something stupid, so we can bomb him to hell again; for good.

I found a blackbird with a hurt wing in the garden yesterday. Managed to rescue it before our Minnie could finish it off; and took it to Mum. She gave me a grin. She was quite amazingly pleased with me.

'Why, Tom,' she said. 'You're getting as bad as Figgis!' Then she added, with a little distracted frown, 'I mean like he used to be. When he was younger.'

And somewhere, from the furthest corner of my memory, I saw the old Figgis giving me his old look of approval.

Robert Westall
The Stones of Muncaster Cathedral

Two chilling stories of the supernatural.

Evil is leaking from the stones of Muncaster Cathedral, and something inside is stirring. Over the years, how many victims has the dark presence in the south-west tower claimed? Reawakened one more, it's hungry to kill ...

Harry Shaftoe's lodging hide a sinister secret. Can a girl be reaching out of the war to him, from the blazing heart of the London blitz? Mesmerised and obsessed, how far will Harry go to satisfy her remorseless appetite?

Robert Westall
Urn Burial

Up on Fiend's Fell, Ralph stumbles over the stones of a cairn and finds the coffin of a creature from another world. Terrfied and excited, he hides his discovery thinking no one will ever find it.

But it's too late. The signal has been sent.

Ralph and his quiet Pennine village become caught up in a deadly battle between alien species. Alone and afraid, what can he do again the invaders and the horrifying weapon they hold, capable of destroying the entire human race?

'a strong, well-written encounter with the supernatural'
Daily Telegraph

'pounds along from one heart-stopping moment to the next'
TES

Robert Westall
The Wheatstone Pond

Too many deaths, too many suicides. It was more than coincidence. The Wheatstone Pond was a killer. When it's drained, Jeff Morgan gets interested, hoping there'll be a few valuable wrecks of model boats down there.

But nothing prepared him for what he was going to find.

In the black water and thick mud something is alive, waiting, hungry for new victims. As strange things start to happen, Jeff can fell the darkness creep round him, drawing him deeper into the rotting heart of the Wheatstone Pond ...

'Gutsy and energetic, grippingly plotted ... inspiringly moral and compassionate.' *Guardian*

Robert Westall
Falling into Glory

Seventeen-year-old Robbie has brilliant exam results and a history of triumphs on the rugby field – until develops a close relationship with a teacher, Emma Harris.

For Robbie, school, sport, and his family begin to lose their importance – but what does Emma want? Is she prepared to risk her whole career for him?

Together they take an Icarus flight almost too near the sun.

Robert Westall
The Kingdom by the Sea

Winner of the Guardian Children's Fiction Award

Mam and Dad were taking their time getting to the shelter tonight. What was keeping them? The Jerry as getting closer. Where were they? And then the whistling scream of bombs. Harry began to count. If you were still counting at ten, the bombs had missed you. The last thing he remembered saying was 'seven'.

The bomb destroys Harry's home and family. Alone in the world, he knows he'll be sent off to live with fussy Cousin Elsie. His life would be a misery. Like the stray dog he meets on the beach, Harry must keep running to be free.

Harry fights for his survival, but there's one last battle he could not prepare for.

'Outstanding'
Guardian

Robert Westall
Harvest

Brian is young, energetic, hungry for the summer.
He imagines Philippa has joined the harvest camp
for some pleasurable nostalgia. The chance to relive
an old affair, perhaps.

But as much as Brian enjoys life, Philippa fears it.
She is fighting to forget a past more terrible than
Brian can imagine.